THIS N.
LIFE

THE MORE A STORY IS TOLD

THE LESS POWER IT HAS

OVER THE PERSON IT BELONGS TO

By

ANNIE HEDLEY

Copyright © Annie Hedley 2021
This book is sold subject to the condition that it shall not, by way of trade or otherwise, be lent, resold, hired out, or otherwise circulated without the publisher's prior consent in any form of binding or cover other than that in which it is published and without a similar condition including this condition being imposed on the subsequent publisher.
The moral right of Annie Hedley has been asserted.
ISBN-13: 9798459577273

This is a work of fiction. Names, characters, businesses, organisations, places, events and incidents either are the product of the author's imagination or are used fictitiously. Any resemblance to actual persons, living or dead, events, or locales is entirely coincidental.

CONTENTS

PROLOGUE 1
1 7
2 12
3 17
4 21
5 26
6 29
7 37
8 43
9 48
10 54
11 59
12 63
13 67
14 74
15 79
16 84
17 89
18 92
19 100
20 105
21 107
22 111
23 117
24 118
25 124
26 127
27 132
28 137
29 142
30 145
31 149
32 155
33 161

34	*164*
35	*167*
36	*172*
37	*176*
38	*180*
39	*186*
40	*191*
41	*195*
42	*202*
43	*205*
44	*211*
45	*214*
46	*217*
47	*222*
48	*230*
49	*233*
50	*244*
51	*248*
52	*258*
53	*262*
54	*267*
EPILOGUE	*273*
ABOUT THE AUTHOR	*278*

PROLOGUE

The usual thought ran through my head in the hospital waiting room. I couldn't help it, it was an old self-conscious habit and hard to kick whenever I had an appointment. Walking into the place had been less of a problem than I had expected, which was a plus. This new building had an entrance on the side of it, discreetly tucked away. All the sign above the door had written on it was 'outpatients', which didn't really indicate anything, other than no one in there had brought their pyjamas and toothbrush with them.

Instead of worrying about the other people in the waiting room and whether they were speculating why I was there, I looked around the room for something to distract me from my paranoia. It was only when I started to read all the stuff pinned on the notice boards and flicked through the leaflets lying around, that I noticed all the information was about the same thing.

Well, what do you know, I thought to myself. *After all these years, I'm finally in the company of others who are here for the same reason I am.*

"Sarah?" someone from a set of double doors called out.

"Yes, that's me," I replied while waving at the woman from my seat and scooping up the minimum three bags I always had with me. One for work, one for food and a handbag large enough to hold the usual necessities plus a spare cardie and an emergency repair kit

1

which was mostly make-up, a few tampons and a packet of breath freshener mints.

If I was stuck in some unforeseen and unfortunate event, I was ready. Life so far had taught me that it wasn't out of the realms of possibility that I'd find myself in yet another shitty situation.

The woman smiled at me warmly and beckoned me to follow her through the double doors.

Here we go, I thought. *Over to the dark side.*

I followed the woman through the doors while considering how much I wanted to say. I was a long way from home so the appointment was with someone I hadn't met before. I had promised myself I wouldn't go over the whole story again, there was no need to. Get back outside in the sunshine as quickly as possible was the plan. Gratefully grab my medication and head for the door.

Once on the other side, the working spaces of the clinic were orderly, functional and eerily quiet. I didn't like the waiting room but at least it had a telly, the familiar sound of Homes Under the Hammer comforting. I walked in time with the woman through an airless artificially lit corridor, turning a sharp left into a small side room.

Still no windows, I thought.

"Blimey," I said to the woman as I walked into the room and looked around it. "You must feel like you work in Hitler's bunker."

The woman smiled again and laughed. She seemed nice.

"I'm Julie, by the way. I'm going to be looking after you today, as it's your first visit," Julie said.

"Sorry," I said, "I sometimes say inappropriate things when I'm nervous. I didn't mean to mention Hitler. Hitler was a dick."

"No, I'm sorry, about the room. I've tried to make it look a bit more inviting and less like somewhere in a hospital," Julie said.

"Yes, I can see that. Very comfy. For a bunker," I said, as I threw her a cheeky sideways glance.

A purple tie-dye throw had been fixed to the wall, the type that might be bought in Camden Market. It served its purpose by deflecting attention from the white walls, even though Indian throws were never going to have anything other than a temporary student accommodation look to them.

In front of the throw were two low bucket-style chairs, one of which I sat on, or in, bucket chairs being what they were. The table in between the chairs had a small lamp on it, softly lighting up the room. Next to it was a box of tissues, one poking out of the top, ready for the plucking if needed. I got the impression if someone were to get upset and cry, this would be a great place for it.

Julie picked up a laminated 'do not disturb' sign off the table. While she pressed the sign onto the outside of the door, fiddling with the Blu-Tack on the back of it, we made pleasant small talk before getting down to business.

"Do you have any idea how long?" asked Julie, tilting her head to one side to make the question seem less intrusive. She wasn't a nurse and quite clearly a therapist. Not what I had expected when I'd made the appointment, but a nice touch, and presumably the protocol with new patients.

"I'm not depressed," I said.

"No, you don't seem to be," Julie replied.

"I can be, if you need me to be. Depressed. If that's what your job is. I can tell by the bunker that's what you're supposed to be, if in here with you."

Such a suck-up people pleaser. Another thing I couldn't help. It was in my nature to want to please.

"You don't have to be depressed to benefit from talking to someone," Julie said.

"I don't need to talk, I'm fine."

"Well that's good. Of course, you don't have to talk if you don't want to."

"It will be eight years next February," I said.

I wanted it to sound as if I was okay with having this anniversary in my life but wasn't sure if I'd pulled it off. It was the small squeak it the middle of "February" that had let me down. Julie looked up from her notepad, puzzled, so I gave her an explanation.

"I know exactly how long I have been living with HIV because I was involved in a criminal investigation that provided me with the answer. The investigation was based on a complaint I made to the police. It resulted in a court case and a conviction."

Julie studied me as she gathered her thoughts. I didn't mind, I was used to being of high interest to HIV professionals. HIV-positive people fascinated them.

The accent must have given it away. That's where I would've put my money, had I been a betting lady.

"Sarah, can I ask you something?" Julie said.

"Yeah, sure," I replied.

"Are you 'X'?"

I raised my eyebrows in surprise at my courtroom alias being mentioned. I hadn't expected to be recognised at all, let alone so quickly.

"You know about all of that?" I asked, still surprised.

"Oh yes, of course. I followed it in the papers as it was happening," Julie replied. "It was big news in HIV circles, how could it not be? You were the first person in the country to successfully prosecute someone under those circumstances. Congratulations," Julie said.

"Um, thanks," I said, not sure what else to say.

"It must have been extremely difficult. You must have gone through a lot of emotional stuff," Julie said.

"I'm not depressed," I said, again.

"No, I know you're not, that's not what I meant. I would love to hear about it, that's all. If you want to tell me, that is," Julie replied.

"I don't want to talk about it," I said.

"That is absolutely fine, I completely understand," Julie said.

Two hours later, I'd told her all about it. And enjoyed it.

"Wow. That's some story," Julie said, sitting back in her seat and putting her hands behind her head, elbows in the air. "Have you ever thought about writing about it?"

"Me? No," I replied.

"Why not? It might help someone to read about your experience."

"Because the longest thing I've ever written is the back page of an application form for a job. Thanks, Julie, but I'm not clever enough."

"I think you'd surprise yourself. It's the way you tell it. If you can capture that on paper it would be incredible to read."

"I'll think about it," I said.

After picking up my bottles of tablets from the pharmacy and stuffing them into my very large handbag, I headed for home. Couldn't get through the door quick enough, was the truth of it.

Bags dumped in the middle of the floor, I turned my laptop on at the kitchen table and an hour later had written the first chapter of my book. I didn't have a name for it, but it would come, in time.

1

There was a summer of some years ago, I decided to treat myself to a holiday romance. It was a straightforward decision, most of mine were. Decision-making came easy to me, I wasn't a ditherer. The path of least resistance was the way my mind worked.

Whatever felt right, I did and when my mind was made up about something, I stuck with it. Consequences didn't come into it but in a good way. My actions were led by a firm belief everything always worked out in the end. One way or another. Robin was a good decision. Meeting him saved my life.

Robin was visiting family he had in England, the summer we met. He was French. We were introduced to each other at a wedding. Robin didn't know the couple getting married, he'd tagged along with his brother. It was easy to gate-crash parties when you looked and sounded like Robin did, the bridesmaids were particularly excited to see him.

"Where's Batman? Getting the round in?" I asked, shaking his hand to avoid an awkward double-cheeked kiss. Robin might have been a Frenchman but where I came from, kissing someone on both cheeks made you a bit of a twat.

"Cheeky English girl," he grinned, good-humouredly.

Later in the evening I wandered outside to get some air and away from Celine Dion. There was only so much of slow-dancing couples a single person could take. Robin must have felt the same way. After a few minutes of standing on my own, he turned up by my side. A brave move, for a person who had only just started to learn how to speak in a different language.

Robin pulled a crumpled packet of cigarettes out of his pocket, offered me one, then stuck a particularly bent one in his mouth. His lips gripped it. My vagina thought it had died and gone to heaven. I watched him and thought rude thoughts.

Robin pointed to the end of his crooked cigarette and said, "I need fire. Can you tell me where the fire is?"

"There's a fire?" I replied, looking around in mock alarm.

"No, not a fire, fire. The fire for this," he said, his finger still pointing at the end of the cigarette.

His unrehearsed English made his accent heavy. It was like a bowl of porridge, thick enough to stick a spoon in and leave standing up, all by itself. It was also delightful and I was enjoying myself. At Robin's expense but he didn't mind in the slightest.

"I don't know if the hotel sells lighters but I'd better ask for you. The receptionist might think you're a, what's the word again? For someone who starts fires for kicks? It's on the tip of my tongue," I said.

"Tip of your tongue?" Robin said slowly.

Take me now, I thought.

"Pyromaniac!" I shouted.

"What is that?" Robin asked.

"Never mind, it doesn't matter," I laughed.

"You are lovely," Robin said, joining in with my laughter, even though he didn't know what he was laughing at.

We liked each other but I knew nothing serious would come of it. As flattering as Robin's interest in me was, it was unrealistic to envisage a relationship would develop between us that would withstand the test of time. It wouldn't get a chance to.

Robin's visit was temporary; he intended to go back to France. He was staying with his brother, who had settled in England some years back after meeting his wife. There was no hurry and no return ticket booked, but Robin would be leaving England and heading for home at the end of his trip.

Living in the moment made the time we had together exciting and getting to know each other became a game we played. I couldn't quite decide which conversations I liked best. The ones that worked well and we understood each other, or the ones that got lost in translation because they were so entertaining. One of the latter could take up a whole Sunday afternoon stroll, the mistakes leading to happy bursts of laughter, much to the amusement of passers-by.

"I used to work in a call centre," I told Robin on one such Sunday afternoon. "I hated it, but it paid for college."

"What is a call centre?" he asked.

"You know, a building with people working in it, usually women."

"Doing what?"

"I was a call handler. The in-house joke was we called ourselves the call girls. They were a nice bunch, if I didn't know what to do with a client, one of the other call girls would take over."

Robin stopped walking, "You mean call girl like prostitute?"

"Yes, exactly. Prostitute. It made the time go quicker. Long days, one client after another and so many dicks to deal with."

There were so many. It would have been hard to pick out my favourite, but Robin thinking I had once been a sex worker was up there with the best of them.

Robin liked to leave cakes on my doorstep. I would arrive home from work to a box of them pressed up against the front door. Part of Robin's courtship routine, I played along. He'd hide around a corner to watch me find them and I would pretend I didn't know he was there.

He left little hand-written notes in the cake boxes, a mish-mash of vocabulary trying to express something meaningful. The words might have been all jumbled up but I knew what Robin was getting at.

"This is terrible, a catastrophe," he said one day as we walked along the beach, all wrapped up because summer was over.

"It's okay, Robin, we knew you'd be going back to France. We'll keep in touch," I said, not wanting him to feel bad about leaving.

"Don't say that, please, Sarah," Robin replied, stopping and holding my face in his hands.

"Okay, we'll not keep in touch."

"Very funny, cheeky English girl. It's not that, I don't have to go. It's something else. I want children, one day, and I think that is probably finished for you."

His departure could be put on hold, unlike me getting any older. Robin was a lot younger than me but it wasn't so much the age gap that mattered, it was what we had done with the difference in our years. I was already a mother and my children were growing up fast.

Robin wanted to be a father and his children were nothing more than a vision in his mind's eye of the way he wanted his future to be. I could see the finishing line as far as my parenting days were concerned. Robin, on the other hand, was still on the starting blocks waiting for the pistol to go off.

"You're right, it's not something I've thought about for a long time. Don't get me wrong, I've loved every minute of it other than when they've driven me mental and thought they were ruining my life."

"What is mental?" Robin asked.

"Nuts," I replied.

"Nuts?" Robin said.

"Yes, but don't ever say that to a nutter because it's not very nice."

"Um, okay," Robin said, giving up trying to understand what I was talking about and keep me on topic which wasn't always easy.

"And children?" he asked, so sincerely if I could've plopped out a half-French baby just for him, there and then, I might have.

"My two are my world, but I don't know if I have any space or time left in it, for any more," I said to Robin, still standing in the same spot as the wind whipped the sand around our feet.

"Maybe in a year? If we are still together and before it's too late?" Robin replied.

"You're not asking for much, are you?" I laughed, turning around to walk back up the beach. "Come on, let's go. It's getting cold."

I had ruled out the idea of having any more children, but I couldn't help thinking about what Robin had said as we walked. It was all so endearing I began to wonder if I could be persuaded.

You never know what's just around the corner, I thought as I smiled to myself.

This was Robin and me, our romance the backdrop to my story.

A drumroll to the main event.

2

Back home and warming up in front of the fire, Robin was on a roll. He wanted to keep on talking about us.

"I'm being serious. I'll stay in England if you want me to. Let's be a couple," he said.

"I thought we were one," I replied.

"Nearly."

"How can you nearly be a couple? What do you do to be a proper couple?"

"Go for an HIV test together."

"An HIV test? Why? I thought we'd got past the business of you thinking I was a prostitute."

"I'm not joking."

"I know you're not, I can tell."

"Don't be offended," Robin said. "It's a compliment. It means you are important to me."

I hadn't been asked to participate in joint HIV testing before. It might have meant Robin wanted to stay with me, which was decent of him, but it wasn't the most Mills and Boon of suggestions I'd ever heard. Discussing HIV and sexual health testing with my new boyfriend was about as comfortable as a trip to the gynaecologist.

I came from a nation of people, who as a rule, shied away from discussing anything too personal. We didn't wear our hearts on our sleeves in the way the French did. British reserve had gained its reputation for a reason and this wasn't necessarily a good thing.

I liked to think it was getting better with each new generation and different for my children because when I was growing up, my parents never talked to me about relationships or sex and viewed nakedness as unnatural.

For years, I thought reproduction had something to do with my digestive tract because my mum's explanation for it was that babies popped out of grown-up's bottoms when they got married. If I came downstairs in my nightie, because I was bare underneath it, I was told to go back to my room and cover up by putting a dressing gown on. It wasn't like I had taken to doing handstands on the front lawn with my vagina in the air, it was simply the rule in our house that everyone wore clothes at all times.

I wasn't convinced my parents had ever seen each other fully naked. Out of them both, my dad was the most committed never-nude. God only knew how they'd managed to have children, it must have been tricky, but my mum must have wrestled him out of his underpants on at least three separate occasions because I had a brother and a sister. There was a tangible difference between a never-nude and a nearly-nude. Three kids.

My parents had once told us, they were thinking about donating their bodies to medical science to save us the cost of their funerals after they'd gone. In a bid to make them reconsider, I told them it would be awful not to have anything left of them to lay to rest, once the anatomy students had finished with them.

It wasn't so much their offspring's distress at the thought of them being sliced open on surgical slabs that changed their minds. Even when I told my mum her head would be chopped off, it didn't bother her that much. What swayed it, after I had pointed it out, was that they would be stared at for three whole years with no clothes on.

Robin's outlook was different to mine. He was younger, his attitude unstifled by rules of so-called social convention. If couples were serious about each other they went for an HIV test together. That meant someone had to broach the subject and Robin was perfectly comfortable with this being him.

Whether it was about getting me pregnant or HIV, Robin was a straight talker, he didn't mince his words. It could have been he didn't have enough extended English vocabulary to present his thoughts with a little more eloquence or that he was in a hurry to get on with forging out a future together. Whatever the reason, Robin's directness was refreshing. Not unlike having a bucket of ice-cold water poured over my head at times, but nevertheless, a change from the usual fudging around the edges most people did with delicate subjects.

To demonstrate what a run-of-the-mill event going on one of these joint HIV testing excursions was, Robin described how it worked.

Couples booked appointments and went together. When the results arrived confirmed in writing, as previously agreed upon by both parties, they showed the letter to each other. It was like an unprotected sex prenup. They could then have worry-free sex to their heart's content or children if they so desired. Amongst the sensible people of France, this was the undisputed drill when embarking on a relationship that looked like it was going somewhere. It was the grown-up thing to do.

What a good idea, I thought, once I got past my initial uneasiness about the subject. I wished I'd heard of it some other time in my adult life, because now I had to tell Robin I'd never been for an HIV test. I had only attended family planning clinics, as they were called back in the day for just that, to make sure I had no more babies.

Everything Robin had said made so much sense, I felt embarrassed admitting HIV testing had never crossed my mind. When he asked why not, I told him the only thing I could think of to say. I didn't know anyone who was HIV-positive. Robin shook his head while he stated his disapproval in no uncertain terms.

"It isn't my fault I happen to be British and we hate talking about anything other than the weather," I said, to lighten the mood.

After the telling off I received from Robin, I couldn't get to the nearest sexual health clinic quick enough, to shut him up. Our appointments were arranged and we arrived at the clinic together. The medical staff who attended to us individually knew we were a couple.

Once in separate rooms, the nurse I was with needed to complete a form regarding the reason I had requested HIV testing. I got the impression the paperwork was necessary because a solid reason was expected when someone asked for the test. I didn't have one, other than Robin.

"Have you had a sexual relationship with anyone from the continent of Africa?" the nurse asked without looking up from her tick list.

"No," I answered.

"Have you shared a needle with a drug user?"

"No."

"Have you ever paid for sex or been paid for sex?"

"No."

"Have you had unprotected sex with anyone in the last year?"

"No."

"How many sexual partners have you had in the last year?"

"Including Robin?"

"Yes."

"One."

The nurse looked up from her list. "Then I'll have to write something in the 'other' category. Why are you here?"

I apologetically told her I didn't suspect I was at risk of anything, let alone HIV.

"It was the boyfriend's idea. He's French," I said as if that explained it all.

My blood sample taken, I left the room quickly to let the nurse get on with seeing to the next person on her appointment list, a person who might have legitimately needed an HIV test.

I was more worried about being a time-waster than HIV-positive.

3

In non-urgent cases, it took a few days to receive HIV test results. I had requested a response in the post because I wouldn't need to talk to anyone about my expected negative result.

A week after visiting the clinic with Robin, I was working from home on a Friday afternoon. I noticed a missed call and a voicemail message left on my mobile from earlier in the day.

"Hi Sarah, my name is Eve. Can you call me back on the following number as soon as possible please?" the voice said. I didn't know anyone called Eve.

The message made me feel slightly nervous. The lack of information was disconcerting and the voice sounded like it belonged to someone with a heavy heart. I checked the number in my contacts list. The call had come from the clinic. This made me feel even more uncomfortable and thoughts started running through my head that I couldn't stop. I didn't understand why someone would call me when I had asked for a letter in the post.

My call went straight to voicemail when I dialled the number, so I hung up, unsure what to say. I waited ten minutes before trying again and when no one answered for the second time, I left a brief message requesting a call back.

I stood and looked out of the window while I waited and watched all the familiar things going on in my street. People getting in or out of their cars with bags of shopping, children on their way somewhere chattering noisily, the postman knocking on a neighbour's door and making their dog bark.

"Is this going to be the end of my life as I know it?" asked the realistic me.

"Get over yourself, silly girl. Of course it's not. Stop thinking, you know it's bad for you," said the hopeful me.

"Well why would they be calling then?" persisted the realistic me.

"It's obvious. The clinic is saving stamps by calling people, that's all. Stop frightening yourself. Everything's fine," said the hopeful me reassuringly.

I was reassured.

Thank God for that, I thought when the phone eventually rang. *Here comes the good news.*

When Eve spoke, I noticed straight away the expression in her voice matched the message she had left, she still sounded sad. Dread filled me.

"Told you," the realistic me said. *"This is bad. This is going to be very, very bad."*

When Eve asked repeatedly if it was possible for me to come to the clinic to speak to her, I ignored the question and instead begged her to get it over with, to tell me what she needed to say.

Eve said, "Sorry," and I knew.

My HIV test result had come back positive.

I'd never been in shock before. I'd been shocked but not in shock. I was a fainter. The last time I'd fainted, had been not that long ago in Claire's Accessories getting a new ear piercing and I'd made a right show of myself. This felt similar. Suddenly, I was in a spinning sauna.

A hot, steamy, sweaty sauna room, rotating furiously like Dorothy's house in *The Wizard of Oz*. I was stuck in it because someone had locked the door from the outside.

I thought I was going to throw up, I wanted to throw up, but couldn't. My knees buckled as I grabbed the edge of the table I was standing next to for support. The ends of my fingers tingled before turning numb. A high-pitched hissing sound in my head squealed like an old-fashioned kettle whistle, but I could still hear the word, "No," being repeated over and over. It was said in rhythm to a pulse that was pounding throughout my entire body. I knew it was me, but it didn't sound like my voice.

I wet myself. Actually wet myself. Pissed my pants. That's what happened when I got told I was HIV-positive.

"Sarah? Are you alright? Speak to me, please," Eve was saying, at the end of a long tunnel, somewhere in the room.

Worried, she spoke quickly.

"Sarah, can you get to the clinic? Are you okay to drive? We need to see you."

The faster Eve talked the more I slowed down, in every way.

As if glued to the spot I was standing in, I found it difficult to move. My brain couldn't access the part of it that turned thoughts into communication, I couldn't speak to Eve properly because it was still doing catch-up with the information she had just given it. The words either wouldn't come out, or form into a sentence that made sense. I stood, my mouth opening and shutting like a goldfish, the phone still pressed to my ear.

"Just answer me this, are you at home? At the address you gave us?" Eve asked.

My brain gave itself a shake and woke up again.

"I've wet myself," I said to Eve, no tone to my voice.

"Oh God, stay put. I'm on my way. Is that okay?" Eve asked.

"Why? What's going to happen? Do you have to take me somewhere?" I asked back.

"No, not at all. I need to see you. I'll talk to you when I get there."

"Alright. I'll go and get changed because I've wet myself. Have you ever wet yourself, Eve? It's never happened to me before."

"I'm on my way," Eve said and hung up the phone.

HIV was real. It existed. Since the recognition of it as a medical condition in the eighties, a person would've had to have been living on a different planet to not know what HIV was. Authors had written about it. Film production companies had made movies about it.

Being told I had it, was something else entirely different.

Tickets at the ready. All aboard. The HIV Express to my own private version of hell and back was about to depart.

First stop, Shame.

4

When I opened the door to Eve, the first thing I noticed was that she looked proper, in a flight attendant kind of way. There was something about her precisely cut bob and the way she had tied a scarf around her neck that made me feel like asking for a large gin and an extra sick bag.

I bet she's not HIV-positive, I thought to myself as I invited Eve in. *This doesn't happen to respectable people.*

In the short amount of time it had taken Eve to get to me, I had already started to judge people with HIV, even though I was one of them. It wasn't that anything had changed outside, the streets animated with the usual hustle and bustle of life. It was the way I viewed my existence in it that had altered.

Like the quick twist of a kaleidoscope, something bright and colourful had turned dark and murky. Just like that, the world had become a place with only two types of people in it. The ones with HIV and the normal folk.

"I am so embarrassed," I said to Eve as she sat down next to me.

"Don't be. People react to shock in different ways. It's just a wet pair of pants at the end of the day," she said kindly, putting her hand on the top of my nearest shoulder to her, as she spoke.

"What? No, not that, I couldn't have given a fuck if I'd shit myself and then hurled it out the window at a passing car. Chimpanzees do that, don't they? When they're upset," I said.

"You're bound to be feeling all sorts of different things," Eve said, unsure what to say next after my comment on turd throwing.

We sat in silence for a few moments and when the silence became too awkward, for Eve, I was way beyond social niceties, she said, "How are you doing? What are you thinking right now?"

"I am so embarrassed, I wish I was dead. That's what I'm thinking. Because I'm…" I couldn't finish the sentence out loud.

HIV-positive, I thought in my head.

My HIV and I were probably not the type of last appointment Eve would have chosen to have had on a Friday afternoon.

Eve talked, and I tried to listen. Sometimes I talked back but we were out of sync. Eve would be on one subject and I would be on another, my thoughts jumping around erratically. I would barely get past one horror, before another leapt into my brain in its place. I didn't cry, though, it wouldn't come.

"I'm sorry, I need to take a blood sample from you," Eve said eventually, patting the black bag next to her feet.

"Will I have to do this every day now?" I asked while I rolled a sleeve up.

"No. This is for a second HIV test. We do this when we get a positive result back from the lab, to make sure it's definitely right," Eve replied.

"So, there's a chance my test result could be wrong?"

Eve looked at me while she decided what to say next.

"I'm not supposed to say this, but I don't want to give you false hope. When your results came back from the hospital laboratory, the words 'strongly positive' had been hand written and circled at the top of the print-out we get back. As if someone was flagging up your results as a high priority."

"What does that mean? You are either HIV-positive or not, right?" I asked.

"Yes, that's right," Eve said sadly.

She paused, unsure whether to continue.

"Go on," I said, "I need to hear this."

"I know it's early days, but the sooner you start to accept it the better. You've been diagnosed as HIV-positive. The doctor you will be seeing next week, put your file on my desk and told me to contact you immediately. He wants to see you first thing Monday morning."

While Eve took my blood sample, she told me about someone she knew who had ovarian cancer. The point to her story was that things could be worse. Eve would take HIV over ovarian cancer any day of the week. I knew she was just trying to be kind and I wished I felt bad for her friend's ovaries, but I didn't. I was barely listening.

All I could think of was my own dire circumstances and that things couldn't possibly be any worse. However, I still put Eve's offerings regarding ovarian cancer on a mental Post-it note. It would come in handy, later in the day.

Suddenly irritated by her presence, I wanted Eve to leave. She wasn't the reason why I was HIV-positive but she'd been the one who'd told me. I'd had enough of nurses and needles for one day.

"I think I want you to go now," I said, not caring how rude it sounded.

"Are you sure? Do you want to call someone? I don't think it's a good idea for you to be on your own right now," she replied, the concern in her voice clear.

"Why? In case I do off with myself?"

"No, that's not what I was suggesting, I didn't mean…" Eve said, her voice trailing off.

"Tempting, but if I was going to do that, I'd have to think about it first. Make sure it looked like an accident. Save the family any embarrassment."

"I really don't think I should leave you on your own."

"You're not. My boyfriend is going to be here in a minute. It would be better for you to go before he arrives. I want to talk to him on my own."

"Okay, I understand. I'll see you on Monday morning at the clinic then?"

"Yes, you will."

"With your boyfriend?"

"I doubt it."

Eve left, biting her lip and looking back at me as she walked down the garden path. I waved over-enthusiastically from the door, as I shouted, "Cheerio! Lovely to see you! Come again soon!"

Better the neighbours thought Eve was a favourite aunt than an HIV nurse. Not that Eve's appearance gave away any vocational clues other than she might have been an off-duty flight attendant but I was covering all bases anyway.

Her friend's ovaries hadn't got a look in but I felt for Eve once she had left. It had been good of her to be so concerned about me. I suspected clinic staff didn't usually do house calls and as house calls went, mine was up there with a trip to the dentist for a molar root canal.

She must have shuddered all the way back to her car, I thought as I closed the front door behind me. I knew myself well. When I got a certain way, I was no walk in the park.

Feeling sorry for Eve didn't last very long. I needed to press on and get back to the task at hand. One visitor down, another to go.

5

Shortly after Eve's departure, the doorbell rang, and I only opened the door because I knew who was going to be on the other side of it. I needed to get this conversation over with and rid of him as quickly as possible.

Robin stood on the doorstep smiling happily, holding up his now customary end-of-week rose in one hand and bottle of wine in the other.

Yippee, it's the weekend, I thought flatly.

I found it impossible to raise my eyes to look at him because my eyelids had big sacks of shame stuck to them and the effort physically hurt. I indicated that we should go into the kitchen to talk. As I walked Robin followed me, concerned enough by now to ask what was wrong.

"I can't see you anymore," I said.

"Why?" Robin asked.

"I have cancer."

"You have cancer? When did this happen? Since this morning when I left you?"

"Yes, that's correct. A cancer doctor has been out to see me. Just left, actually."

"Where is this cancer?" Robin asked suspiciously.

"In my ovaries."

"What is ovaries?"

"Lady parts. The eggy parts. This means I can't have any more children."

Robin's desire for children had given me the perfect get out clause. I hoped my faked infertility would mean Robin would leave without an argument. Robin stood on the spot staring at me.

"You'll meet someone, Robin. Someone your own age, who can give you children. That would be for the best," I said, red-faced and thoroughly ashamed of myself.

The lie was by far the worst I'd ever told, and I couldn't quite believe I was saying it. A darker shade of white lie, but nevertheless, it was still a whopper. I wasn't proud of it and I wasn't a bad person, just desperate. The time of delivering it and the hour that had preceded it, was the lowest point of my life.

Unsurprisingly, Robin didn't buy it. When he hugged me, I finally cried and told him the truth, which he had guessed anyway.

I let him hold me for a few seconds before pushing him away. Staring at his feet, still unable to look at him, I said quietly, "It's okay, you know, that you will want to go. You can leave, it's fine."

"Why would I want to leave?" Robin gently replied, lifting a hand to try and touch my face.

I took a step backwards so he couldn't reach me. Robin's hand floated in the empty space between us, before he let his arm drop back to his side.

"Why would you want to stay? Why would you want to be

anywhere near me? You must feel repulsed at the thought of it. You don't have to pretend, it's not necessary."

The brief moment of assertiveness wore me out. My chin dropped again, this time touching the intertwined knuckles of my tightly clasped hands placed underneath it.

Choked, a small sob escaped as I spoke. "I am going to ask you for only one thing. Don't tell anyone what you know about me. For my children. Please, I'm begging you."

Robin didn't leave, he insisted on staying, and he said all the right things. This was not a reason to end a relationship, that I was still the same beautiful woman, and everything would be all right.

None of which I believed for a second.

6

Monday morning came around and I was at the clinic hanging out with my HIV crew. Robin, Eve and my newest homie, a doctor who preferred to be called by his first name, which was Alex.

The good news was Robin's HIV test had come back negative, however, he had tested positive for chlamydia and needed to take a little blue tablet to sort out his sexually transmitted disease. On the scale of things, I decided, I was prepared to let it go. As expected, the result of my second HIV test was positive.

Eve might have mentioned the availability and effectiveness of HIV treatment during Friday's house call but if she had, this important piece of information had eluded me completely. My fevered brain had been far too pre-occupied working out how to tell Robin I wasn't HIV-positive, even though I was, and had cancer, even though I didn't. This had mattered more than listening to advice on how to stay alive.

I had spent the entire weekend working on my end-of-life plan and this featured heavily when asked by Alex if I had any questions about my diagnosis.

"Is there anything you would like to talk about or questions you would like answering?" Alex asked calmly.

I looked at Alex and tried to work out how he could be so relaxed when he was talking to a dead woman walking.

"Yes, there is. Just a couple of questions. How long have I got left to live and what will be written on my death certificate?"

High on my long list of horrors was my parents finding out, and if that happened, what it would do to them. My parents were old school. They had met as teenagers, got married, had kids and stayed together. No affairs, no weird shit.

The only time they had ever watched a porno, was when they rented one by mistake 'down at the video shop', as my mum called it, even though it was no such thing. The run-down old corner shop, that sold everything from spaghetti hoops to sanitary towels, had a rack of videos at the back of it available on a 'membership only' basis. My mum was a member and proud of it. She liked showing her friends her membership card at the Thursday tea dance while she chatted on, critiquing all the films she'd watched.

The video they thought they had purchased, turned out not to be the most recent remake of 'Flash Gordon'. They'd forgotten to take their reading glasses with them. Much to my dad's horror at so much nakedness, my mum made him watch 'Flesh Gordon' anyway because if they didn't, it was a waste of the two pounds they'd paid for it.

They were simple, good people, my parents. I loved them dearly and was going to put them through something unimaginably horrible.

As if it wasn't bad enough they had to suffer their daughter's premature death, as if I hadn't caused them enough pain, I was only going to go and die from AIDS. I wasn't sure what dying from AIDS entailed, but if it was confirmed in all its glory on a death certificate, there would be no hiding the fact from my grieving parents.

I was the apple of my dad's eye and God only knew how my mum would cope with the reaction from her church folk. My mum had been born into a non-practicing Methodist family, but she had decided in later years to convert to Catholicism, for the craic.

I couldn't have cared less at the time what faith she favoured, as long as she hadn't joined a dangerous religious cult and was cosying up to some maniac, like a Charles Manson wannabe type of maniac. But I cared now and really wished she hadn't plumbed for the Pope and become a Roman Catholic.

Hell and damnation. That's what her priest would tell her I deserved. The same priest who had talked her into cleaning his house for free and she had gladly done it because she considered it a privilege to scrub someone's toilet who was so Godly. I had lived in mortal sin and paid the price, that's what her man of the cloth would tell her. I couldn't bear the thought of my mum having to put up with other people's unkind words and their open disgust at the mention of my name.

No matter what it took, I was going to make sure my parents did not find out I had been diagnosed with HIV.

I had thought about how difficult it would be to fool the coroner's office that I had something else wrong with me. I was quite taken with the idea of ovarian cancer, but an accidental death would serve equally as well. Drowning was a good one, I lived near the sea. It comforted me to imagine the nice things people would say about me at my funeral. If, I managed to keep my shameful secret from getting out.

"Poor thing. She went for a dip and didn't come back. Such a waste, she was a lovely girl. Clean living."

But I wasn't fussy. All I wanted was my death certificate to state something dignified had finished me off, because AIDS, definitely wasn't that.

Another question I had for Alex distressed me so much, I could barely get the words out past the boulder-sized lump in my throat where my tonsils used to be.

"I also want to know what I should do about my children. Do I need to start preparing them for my death?"

Trying to think about this had taken up a large chunk of my end-of-life planning at the weekend. It had become a very time-consuming exercise. Every time I thought I had a quiet moment to work out how and when to tell my children I was going to die, one of them would come and find me, as children did with their mothers.

Making up an excuse to leave the room, I would find a corner somewhere in the house and cry as quietly as possible, as I thought about leaving the world and therefore my children. The sorrow and pain I felt at not being there anymore to love and protect them, broke my heart. I was overwhelmed with grief, repeatedly. After splashing my face in cold water to hide that I'd been crying, I would do this sad little ritual all over again, a short time later.

Alex and Eve looked surprised at my questions. A common reaction to a new diagnosis may have been to get straight on the internet and find out what it all meant but I hadn't done that. I'd been far too busy. It was news to me that HIV could be controlled and didn't necessarily mean the end of the life of a person who had contracted it.

"Really?" I asked, head tilted to one side.

"Yes and because of treatment, people are living much longer," Eve said.

"How long?"

"We don't know how the condition will affect the bodies of older people so I can't tell you that, there aren't any survivors past a certain age to study yet. That's changing though, because of medication."

"So, there's a chance I'll live longer than my parents and they'll never know?"

"There is every likelihood you will live a near-normal life span and natural order will run its course. HIV is now viewed by professionals as a chronic illness that can be managed if it's detected early enough, rather than a terminal condition."

"What about my children, do I need to tell them?"

"Telling your children isn't something you have to do, if that is your choice."

Death certificates were not so easily explained. Eve tried to smooth the way, but there was no getting around the fact that statements such as 'AIDS-related illness', or 'complications due to AIDS' appeared on the documents presented to the families of HIV patients.

"They don't understand! That's not fair!" I said to Eve.

"No, they don't, and no, it isn't," she agreed.

Alex took over. He knew I was upset and knew what to say. He'd had this conversation before.

"I think, in time, this will be addressed. You are not the first person to ask that question, a lot of people feel the same way. In my opinion, what should be recorded is the reason why a person stopped living at the point of death, the same as everyone else," Alex said.

"So, let's say, I was riding my bike too close to a clifftop and went over the edge. I fell in the sea and drowned or if the tide was out, smashed my skull wide open on a rock. With a bit of luck, that would be put on my death certificate and AIDS wouldn't be mentioned?" I asked, feeling it was a fair enough question to ask an HIV doctor.

"Not exactly, I was thinking more the usual reasons for a person's death," Alex said slowly while rubbing the underneath of his chin and looking at me.

"What are the usual reasons?" I asked, persisting in my line of questioning because Alex wasn't delivering nearly enough information to satisfy my need for a no frills or fussing answer to my question.

"Well, organ failure," Alex said hesitantly and looking mildly uncomfortable.

"Got it. You mean like dropping down dead from a plain old heart attack. That would work for me. I'd be more than happy with that on my death certificate."

"Look. Try not to dwell on it. This isn't something you should be thinking about right now. You've been diagnosed and that means something can now be done. When you need treatment, we can help," Alex said assertively and wrapping the conversation up.

I was convinced. I believed them. If I wasn't going to die anytime soon then it would be safe to let myself start feeling better, even though I could see a flowchart pinned to the wall over Alex's shoulder, that informed staff of what to do if they suspected an HIV patient was suicidal.

Alex needed to do his next job and this one was all about my blood. He needed to take a good look at it to determine where my immune system stood versus HIV. This was fighting talk. My body was now a battlefield.

Alex spoke in a whole new language when talking about HIV. His enthusiasm for his chosen subject and specialist field was admirable but didn't make what he was describing any more palatable. I didn't want to be an HIV patient any more than anyone else on the planet. I paid attention because I had to and kept it as simple as possible for myself, as I listened to what I was being told.

CD4 cells were good. HIV cells were bad. The CD4 count needed to be as high as possible to outnumber and fight the virus. Alex called it my viral load, which made it sound like constipation and I was all bunged up with something nasty. The closer to non-existent the viral load was, the better. Counts and the loads, that was the way of it, and it all sounded hideously unattractive.

"Antiretroviral treatment stops HIV cells replicating and creating more of the virus, but it doesn't necessarily need to start straight away. It could be years before you need medication. Everyone is different. Your CD4 count could still be acceptably high and it's just a case of monitoring it," Alex explained.

More of my beautiful bright red blood was taken, put into specimen tubes and labelled with yellow stickers. Eve wrote my name on the stickers, on a line that had words typed in bold underneath it.

'Caution: highly contaminated', the words declared in no uncertain terms and my diminishing self-esteem disintegrated a bit more at the sight of my name next to them. The little yellow stickers said it all. A statement of the sum total of my worth as a person. It didn't matter what I had achieved in the past. Now, all that mattered, was what I had become.

In my new life, I was unclean. Soiled. Regardless of my well-kept appearance, on the inside, I was toxic and polluted. I pictured a smelly old canal system inside me instead of healthy veins and arteries, empty plastic pop bottles, cigarette butts and duck poo floating about in it.

As I stared at the yellow stickers, my mind wandered to the organ donation card I carried on me and getting rid of it. My organs and my blood were worthless. Worse than worthless. They were infected and dangerous to the normal folk.

Who in their right mind would want a part of me inside them? Might as well be done with it and throw all of me on the rubbish dump, I thought miserably.

Robin and I were free to leave once Eve had spoken to me separately.

"It doesn't matter whether Robin is in the room or not because most of the time he doesn't understand what I'm talking about," I said to Eve, not particularly wanting to be alone with her because of the scary stuff she said.

"What are you talking about?" Robin said to both of us, looking from one to the other.

"See?" I said to Eve.

"Sarah, please," Eve said patiently.

"Convenient, if you are about to ask me what I think you are. I can discuss my sluttyness in front of my boyfriend and he won't have a clue."

Eve held her position.

"Just a quick word in private," she insisted, as she walked out the room and beckoned me to follow.

I slowly walked after her as if wading through mud. It felt like I was drowning in sexual health quicksand after the conversations that had taken place and another one was about to start.

I knew I hadn't done anything wrong, but I also knew what was coming next and it made me feel wretched. Eve was going to ask me about the next thing on the list of horrors in my new life.

Past partners who could be at risk of HIV infection because of me.

7

I lived in the small town where I grew up.

In my town, like many other small towns, everybody knew everybody. People often stayed lifelong friends with childhood pals. I knew married couples who had met in school. People tended to stay put, perfectly content to live out their lives next to the family and friends they saw on a regular, if not daily basis. Social networks were large and bonds were strong. By the nature of small-town life, it was not uncommon to know other people's relationship histories and who was dating who. Some people had dated the same person, and in my town, that was okay.

People socialised in all the same places. They chatted to each other in the same supermarkets, walked their dogs in the same parks and gathered at the gates to collect their children from the same school they went to. My children were taught by teachers I could remember from my school days because they had never moved away or changed their jobs.

It was impossible to walk down the street in my town and not bump into someone I knew. Being in a hurry did not necessarily curtail conversations. Where I came from people liked to talk to each other.

I loved growing up and living in my town, surrounded by people I had known most of my life. In many ways, small town life was enchanting for all the reasons that made the community spirit so strong.

However, in certain circumstances, it had its drawbacks.

Eve did not want to have this conversation and I knew the reason why. This didn't make things any easier for individuals struggling with a new diagnosis; in fact, it made it a whole lot harder.

I understood why it had to be done, but that didn't stop my mind from yet again going into freefall over the rapid and continuing decline of my life. If I couldn't stop the drop; the goo that had once been me, would be found pooling at the bottom of it. All that was left of me bobbing about on the surface. A pair of staring, fearful eyeballs, kept afloat by a pair of Primark knickers.

My blood test results when back from the hospital laboratory, would provide Alex and Eve with some indication of how long I had unknowingly been living with the virus for. This data was not unequivocal, but it was somewhere to start. Eve would use this information as a guide for what she called partner notification. This was basically a confidential process used to track down any other people that could be HIV-positive.

A part of Eve's job was to ascertain if a new patient had any past or present partners that could be unaware they had contracted the virus, at risk themselves of serious health implications and potentially perpetuate the transmission of HIV in the population. As intervention strategies went, it was far from perfect, but until there was a vaccination there was no other way to do it.

Eve explained with an example that made it seem ever so straightforward.

"If your results indicate you have had the virus for five years, ideally any partners within that time frame should be contacted and offered an HIV test. If it is less, all the better. Five years is a good place to start as it covers any margin of error. Most people after that amount of time, will have started to display symptoms of undiagnosed HIV and health issues as a result of it."

It sounded logical and sensible. *So, what's the problem?* I asked myself. *Why do I feel so worried?*

This was the problem.

As I listened to Eve a very scary scenario ran through my mind. It was all in the headcount. One old boyfriend invited for an HIV test probably wouldn't have mattered, but any more than that, the situation got precarious and I got clammy just thinking about it.

I imagined two of my old flames with their negative test results down the pub celebrating, regaling their ordeal of being called for an HIV test and their narrow escape. Someone they knew was HIV-positive and this would be big news in a small town. Like a horrendous game of pairs, the cards would be turned over until there was a match.

"They both went out with her, remember? That can only mean one thing."

I could hear it now, the gossip.

It wouldn't take long before people felt tempted to make connections, and whether their assumptions were correct or not, the whispering and finger pointing would start. It was human nature and life in a small town, where everybody knew everybody.

I had already met and shaken hands with Shame and today he had brought along a good friend of his.

Hello Fear.

These two went way back. The best of pals, they enjoyed each other's company so much, they were inseparable and together made a formidable team.

My children were everything to me. Everything.

They had never given me a day's worry and were working hard to achieve grades at school that would eventually get them into university.

My life may have been finished but over my dead body, was I going to allow my children's lives to be affected by a predicament that was entirely my fault. They were blameless innocents and the guilt I felt over how this could impact on their young lives was devastating.

School ground taunts and childhood trauma, all because of me. Thoughts of people being cruel to them exploded through my brain like a bullet going in one side and out the other. I needed to come up with a plan that included protecting my children from anything that could hurt them.

Over a reasonably large timespan more than covering the five years suggested by Eve, my relationship history consisted of one significant relationship of years rather than months, and since then, four more that had lasted months rather than years.

The longer one had turned out to be a waste of time, and the following three had been with men recovering from a break-up with a former partner, and therefore not much better. The unhappy separation anxiety trio had the same name, which was odd and made me wonder if practically every male child born in the sixties was called Gary.

I referred to the first one as Gary Oldman when it ended and I started dating the second Gary, who I called Gary Numan in secret, just for the fun of it. By Gary number three I couldn't think of any more famous Garys that fit the joke so he just became known as

Gorgeous Gary amongst my friends. It wasn't that they found Gary Oldman or Gary Numan physically repulsive, they assured me, it was just that Gorgeous Gary gave them the proper fanny gallops.

Having heard enough about ex-girlfriends to last a lifetime, it finally dawned on me, I was the rebound relationship. After the third time it happened, I decided I needed to apply a 'two-year rule' when dating, to avoid being the mopper-upper of yet another person's failed relationship and wounded heart.

The rule was, when dealing with people who had been dumped, if they hadn't worked through one year of wallowing in it and another getting over it, leave them to it. Otherwise, they'd just end up crying on your shoulder and shouting out in their sleep, "Tina, take me back, I'm lost without you," while you lay there thinking, *Yeah, for fuck's sake, Tina, do me a favour and take him back.*

I finally learnt my lesson after the relationship I had with Gorgeous Gary came to an end. Unfortunately for me, I had fallen for him and went out with the fourth man on my list, on the rebound. He wasn't called Gary, surprisingly, but it was a near miss because his brother was.

In truth, I'd never had a very long-term relationship, even though I would have described myself as a relationship person. Most people I knew by my age had achieved at least one relationship that had lasted a good ten years or more, but not me. Maybe I wasn't equipped for it or had never met the right person.

I liked the idea of commitment but could never quite manage it. One-night stands and all that malarkey were not for me, that was for sure, but I was a relationship flibbertigibbet. Sometimes I recycled old boyfriends when I wanted company because I couldn't be bothered with the hassle of starting from fresh with a new one. It was terrible, really. In my community, relationship-wise, I was probably considered one hot mess.

Not that any of this mattered now. Part of my plan was to remain unattached and celibate for the rest of my existence in this hostile environment of a planet that didn't feel like home anymore. This was my new life so I had better get used to it because I was doing it on my own. This bit of it at least, I was still in control of.

I told Eve about Mark, the other half of the significant relationship that had ended a few years earlier. It wouldn't be difficult to contact Mark, I told her, he lived in town and his business was on the high street. I knew Mark well enough to be confident he wouldn't mention to anyone he had been contacted by a sexual health clinic, it wasn't his style. Eve wrote on a pink index card as I talked, double checking she'd written the phone numbers down correctly that I'd given her.

As for the others, I wanted to deal with them myself, once I had worked out how to. Eve didn't like this idea one bit, but I had decided it was the best way forward, given where I lived. I needed to avoid two old boyfriends going for tests at the same time, who frequented the same pubs or played football on the same local team. Living in a small town made this perfectly possible.

I got ready to leave the clinic and collected up my coat, bags, and Robin, leaving Eve to make her phone call to Mark. It was Monday morning and I had to get to work.

"What happens next?" I asked her on my way out.

"I'll be in touch when your blood test results are back from the lab. Until then, try not to worry too much. You appear to be fit and well. You'll be fine."

8

My diagnosis begged an obvious question.

Had there ever been any indication I was HIV-positive?

I wondered about possible tell-tale signs I had overlooked or given myself more plausible explanations for, while I mulled the question over in my head. I dismissed things I had started to notice because I wasn't ill and didn't feel any different. On the contrary, I could still run for miles and enjoyed it. I loved running, I always had, as far back as I could remember. I asked myself, if my fitness level because of this had lulled me into a false sense of security regarding my health.

When I ran, I felt alive. I liked the pain. My heart thumping and lungs expanding in my chest reinforced that I was strong and healthy. The endorphins my body released might have been the reason why I felt so happy when I ran, but the strong sense of achievement at the end of a particularly long one was equally as pleasing. Being good at running was physically demanding and took a lot of determination. I could push myself harder than most women I knew half my age and because of this, I felt at the top of my game when I pulled my trainers on for a morning run along the beach.

I was so convinced my health was anything but compromised, I didn't worry about issues that had started cropping up with my skin, that hadn't been there before.

Periodically, my face would flush for a few days. Burning hot as if I had a temperature, my cheeks down to my jawbone would turn bright red as if sunburnt. A girl with perfect skin at a very expensive skincare salon told me it was rosacea. I left with some tubes of face cream that seemed rather pricey, given the amount of stuff that was in them.

I read up on it and found that the cause of rosacea was unknown but flare-ups could happen at any time in a person's life and out of the blue. A lot of things could activate the condition, from stress to sunlight, and the list of triggers was long and random. On it, I noticed, there were a lot of things I enjoyed.

A hot bath, spicy food, red wine and the one that really stood out, strenuous exercise. I thought my research had provided me with the answer. I didn't want to give up any of my favourite things but I could be sensible about it. I could limit some – spicy food and red wine, and avoid others. Showers it was, after a run. I would miss unwinding in a bubble bath, but if it calmed down the rosacea I thought I had, it was worth it.

The skin under my fingernails had become unusually dry and flaky, the line to the nail bed jagged as if something had aggravated the normal healthy pink curves. I promised myself I would always use gloves when cleaning in the house and started using hand cream every time I washed my hands. I guessed the chemicals in the cleaning products were the cause of the irritation to my hands and I just needed to look after them a bit more.

My mouth was another weird one. After a trip to the dentist to repair an old filling, the corners of my mouth were sore. The slight splits that appeared healed up after a couple of weeks, only to reappear every now and again. Annoyed, I thought the dentist had over-stretched my mouth during the procedure and permanently damaged the skin.

My hair was different too, thinner and not as shiny as it once was. I started having it cut a lot shorter than I preferred, in an attempt to thicken it up again. My skin, hair and nails all seemed to be playing up. The keratin I usually had in abundance, seemed to be diminishing but I wasn't overly concerned. It wasn't exactly life threatening or Kaposi's Sarcoma.

When I went to see the doctor, it wasn't because of my skin issues, I didn't consider them serious enough to mention. It was because of enlarged tonsils that had developed out of nowhere and were blocking up the back of my throat. Referred to an otolaryngologist, I was booked in for a tonsillectomy.

Although there were no visible signs of cancer or anything else out of the ordinary, a biopsy was performed on my tonsils to make sure. The result confirmed the absence of any cancerous cells and the problem was simply put down to good old-fashioned strep throat. I thought the streptococcal infections and my stressed-out, keratin-deficient skin were related and due to my busy life. I was run down, more rest and a course of vitamins, that's all I thought I needed.

Youthful looks were a family trait. People often mistook us for being younger than our actual years. The youth gene came from my mother. I remembered growing up and wondering why her nickname amongst friends was 'Peter Pan'. He was a boy, I didn't see how this was a compliment. I realised as I got older it was because she never seemed to age. My mum had remained inconceivably young looking all her life and modestly put it down to rubbing Vaseline into her laughter lines.

I didn't feel any different but I had noticed, I was starting to look it. I didn't look ill, but I looked tired. I seemed to be losing the fresh-faced complexion that I'd been lucky enough to have all my life and for the first time ever, I looked my real age.

I started to suspect my appearance had something to do with my tonsillectomy, particularly due to the unusual length of time it took me to recover from the procedure.

I thought because my tonsils were part of my lymphatic system, removing them had altered the function of my immune system and it wasn't working so well. I wondered if my lacklustre skin and hair were the result of toxins not being removed from my body properly. Whatever toxins looked like, green and spikey came to mind, some of them were still floating around my body making a nuisance of themselves. It didn't get me down though, I had every faith my body would put itself right and all it needed was an adjustment period following the operation.

After missing tonsils, the other reason I gave myself was actual tiredness. I didn't suffer from exhaustion or anything as dramatic as that but I was well aware, I had a lot on my plate. I had a responsible job with a duty of care towards people who used the services I managed, a house to run and a family of my own. It often felt like I was looking after everyone else and no one was looking after me.

Not that I was the pity-party type, but when I looked in the mirror I wondered if this was the reason why my good fortune on the young-looking stakes seemed to be running out. I was getting older and unlike my sister and mother, it was catching up with me and starting to show.

When I was diagnosed with HIV, I was confounded how I couldn't have known there was something seriously wrong with me, even though I hadn't been completely off the mark with the tonsillectomy theory. I'd wanted to rule out throat cancer by asking for a biopsy on my removed tonsils, but HIV never entered my head.

When Eve told me, it was a shock. A real shock. The news traumatised me. I was utterly unprepared for it, but the upside was, I knew. The part I tried not to think about too much was, what would have happened had I not met Robin and found out.

9

After a couple of weeks of relative nothingness, I received the expected call from Eve. She sounded in a hurry and didn't want to get into much of a conversation over the phone. This suited me just fine. It wasn't that I didn't like Eve, she seemed a nice enough person, I just didn't like the things she told me. It wasn't her fault, but it would have been difficult to associate Eve with anything other than bad news.

"Can you come to the clinic this afternoon please? Your results are back, and Alex wants to see you," Eve asked.

"It's alright, Eve. I'm at work and don't mind talking over the phone," I replied.

"It would be better if you could come to the clinic to speak to Alex. Come after work, that's fine. We'll be here."

Eve's voice filled me with a familiar sense of dread.

"Everything is alright, isn't it? With my blood test results?" I tentatively asked.

Eve sighed deeply, struggling with what to say next. "You need to come to the clinic, Sarah. Unfortunately, your results are not what we were expecting."

When I arrived at the clinic Eve tried to hide it, but I could tell she'd been waiting for me. She took me straight to see Alex, who looked serious and concerned. The atmosphere felt heavy with prevailing bad news. Bad news was something I knew about, I recognised it.

"I want you to go straight to a pharmacy to get the tablets and start taking them right away," Alex said, handing me a prescription for three months' worth of heavy-duty antibiotics.

I tried to stay calm by telling myself Alex was being overcautious.

"I don't see why that's necessary. I'm not sick," I said, all pretendy hoity-toity.

"I mean right away, Sarah. Not tomorrow, today," Alex replied.

"I don't want to take a whole load of tablets every day. I'm not a sick person, look at me, do I look ill to you?" I argued.

Alex sat back in his chair and looked at me in silence. He didn't want to frighten me, but I could see he was frightened for me. This, more than anything he had said, terrified me. He put his pen down slowly and swivelled around from his desk, wheeling over to me in his chair until we were eye to eye, knees practically touching. My neck in the same position, I moved my head back. I liked my personal space even if it meant giving myself a double chin.

Eyeballs practically out on stalks, I listened to Alex.

"I am surprised you have not already been admitted into hospital. You are at risk of being seriously ill. Your immune system is so weak, it's almost non-existent. If you choose not to do as I say, you will die."

You. Will. Die.

Each word hit me separately with the power of an invisible physical force punching me in the chest. When I put them all together, I could barely breathe.

"Why are you arguing with him? You are one stubborn pain in my ass. If you could just shut the fuck up and listen for once in your life, this is a good time for it," said the realistic me.

"It's my body. I know her better than anyone else. I trust the old girl, she's done me proud all these years," said the hopeful me, as I patted myself gently on the chest in the way an owner of a beloved car would on the bonnet of his trusty four-wheeled friend.

"Oh, piss off with that shit. Do you want to survive HIV?" asked the realistic me.

"Yes, of course I do," the hopeful me replied.

"In that case, listen to the doctor sitting in front of you whose business it is to know what he is talking about."

The quantity of the virus in my viral load test had measured in the millions which meant the HIV cells in my body were out of control. Or in control, was the other way of looking at it.

My CD4 cell count was way below what Alex had initially anticipated. The cells in my immune system were being destroyed by HIV which meant it wouldn't be able to work properly. My body was under attack and susceptible to cancers and other diseases, wide open to infections usually dealt with efficiently by a healthy immune system.

Antibiotics would help protect my respiratory system from infection and risk of pneumonia. I would start antiretroviral treatment immediately in an attempt to raise my CD4 count because what was left of my immune system was not enough to fight off any serious opportunist infections.

For the rest of my life, I would take tablets every day at the same time because the HIV drugs had to be constantly in my system. Set an alarm clock, put a note on the fridge door, tie a knot in a handkerchief or a red ribbon on the dog's collar. Whatever it took to remember, I had to make sure I did not miss taking a tablet because if I did, the medication would stop working and lots of terrible things would start happening to my body.

Alex wouldn't leave the room until I'd promised him I would be fully compliant, as he called it, with treatment. He then left me in the company of Eve, which meant it was her turn to talk to me about the things women talked to other women about. The opposite sex and what we got up to with them, neither of which I wanted anymore to do with.

When Eve spoke, she didn't sound like Eve the Sexual Health Practitioner, she sounded like Eve the Parole Officer.

"I am under professional obligation to make sure you understand, you have to make sure you do not infect another person with HIV. You are extremely virulent and therefore categorised as a high risk to others. You must not have unprotected sex with another person. If you conceal your HIV status and pass on the virus, you could be prosecuted and serve a custodial prison sentence," she said, all in one go.

I would've been in a hurry too, had it been me having to say that lot, I thought when Eve stopped talking. There was no way of sugar coating what she had just said. My body was now not only offensive, it was criminally offensive.

"Look after yourself, put yourself first," Eve said when she started talking again, back to being the kind HIV nurse.

"Too late for that. It's not like you can get it twice," I said in an overly chirpy voice, weirdly desperate to get a gag in and lighten the mood and conversation, as was my want.

"Well, here's the thing. You can," Eve said.

Apparently, lightening did strike twice.

There were some things that could happen twice and that was okay.

Watching a box set twice was okay.

Being late for work twice was okay.

Dating the same person twice was okay.

Even getting married and divorced twice was reasonably okay.

The first time I'd been too young. The second was in Las Vegas on a ludicrous whim. Not great, but no serious harm done.

Unlike HIV superinfection, given half a chance.

HIV superinfection occurred when some unfortunate soul acquired a second strain of the virus from another person, a different one from their first HIV-positive partner. The bad luck bestowed on a person for this to happen was mindboggling, but it had, because someone had given it a name.

Catching HIV twice was best avoided. The second strain co-existed quite happily with the first, more than happy, fucking ecstatic was more like it. They were such a good match, together they were stronger and resistant to medication. There was only one outcome if this were to happen to an already HIV-positive person. Rapid disease progression and death.

"Please consider everything I've said and protect yourself, from any further health issues and problems," Eve said, sincerely.

"Funnily enough, Eve, dashing out the clinic doors to trawl the streets and find someone to have casual sex with, is not in the forefront of my mind," I said, straight faced and sombre.

"You're still a woman, and a very attractive one at that," Eve said, wanting to finish on a less unpleasant note.

"No, I'm not," I replied.

It all sounded so ugly. I wondered how I'd ever thought sex was normal because all this shit wasn't.

A stay of execution, that's what it felt like. HIV was the hangman's noose and I was living on borrowed time. Not once but twice, I thought I was going to die and it was now all getting a bit much.

I wanted to go home. I felt tired, more tired than I'd ever felt before. I wished I could curl up in my bed for a few weeks because all I wanted to do was sleep.

I imagined waking up to find I was me again, the old me, because all of this had been nothing more than a horrible nightmare, forgotten the moment I opened the curtains and let the sunshine in.

10

Sam was born nine months after me and his dad had done it just the once. As in, just the once without thinking about contraception. He was my lost-in-the-moment baby, and I loved him from that moment onwards. It was kind of cool to know exactly where and when he was conceived.

I hadn't known Pete, Sam's dad, very long when I fell pregnant and we did it all backwards. We had a baby, then moved in together, had another baby, then got married.

We had a very grown-up life for two young people and mostly didn't have a fucking clue what we were doing.

I had the morning sickness curse that lasted all day, every day. It was to become a proper condition with a proper name, Hyperemesis Gravidarum, but in my day chucking your guts up continually just meant you were a soft shite.

My favourite Hyperemesis Gravidarum story of all time was my melon and bananas one. Pete was on house arrest after Sam was born and I was pregnant again with our second child. I had wanted another baby, a girl this time. I had put my order in and Pete had approved it.

Pete's brother was in town, so he was allowed a pass out. I'd manage, I told him. My Hyperemesis Gravidarum was so bad, I couldn't bear anything with an aftertaste. Anything with a bit of flavour to it came back up like hot coals, scorching my insides all the way up. I was starving all the time, in a constant cycle of eating and puking.

Obsessed with what would come up or stay down, I thought about food a lot and decided fruit was the way to go. Pete left for his night out, the lucky bastard; what I would've given to trade places for just one night of alcohol and drunk cigarette smoking with mates. After he'd shut the door behind him, I ate four bananas and a whole honeydew melon for dinner. Ravenous, I pushed the pieces of fruit in my mouth, confident the blandness of it all would ensure it would stay put in my stomach.

When it all came back up, I just made it to the bathroom door. The look I'd gone for in there, was framed prints in different sizes covering all walls above the dado rail. I projectile vomited, covering the whole bathroom including those prints that I had lovingly collected, framed and meticulously hung in a fashion that made it look like they'd been slung up. It had taken ages and I was proud of my bathroom walls.

The bubbly slime ran down the glass on the front of all the pictures and dripped onto the floor from their corners. Then the baby started crying and I joined in. Pete was back home an hour after he'd left.

"What have you been up to? Some redecorating?" he asked, smiling.

"Don't," I said, cuddling Sam and pushing my face into his sweaty little neck to blow false farts and make him giggle.

Pete rolled up his sleeves and scooped a cloth out of the bucket at his feet.

"Go and put the telly on, I'll deal with this. If I can't, I'll call Ghostbusters."

Breastfeeding was another messy affair. No one tells you that when you give birth.

"You can control your flow," they said.

"I can control my flow," I therefore told myself, when trying on post-pregnancy clothes in the what-were-once fashionable horrendous communal changing room of a clothes shop. "Just don't think about hungry, crying babies."

There. I'd done it. Put the picture and sound in my head.

Well that's bullshit, I thought as I snapped around from the maddening crowd of women shopping in the sales and spray painted an impressively straight double line on the mirror-covered wall with breastmilk.

I didn't know if this was something that had happened before, I suspected not because a lot of things that happened to me did not seem to happen to other people, but the girl at the changing room door came rushing over as quick as you like, with glass cleaner and tissue paper.

"What a waste," she said as she wiped the mirrors as quickly as she could.

"I did it on purpose," I said.

The girl turned around and shot me a look, chuckling.

"I do it in all the shops I go in but don't usually get caught. It's my thing."

I needed caesarean sections to deliver both my children safely. Sam was an emergency because he was a breech baby. After a long painful labour, they knocked me out to get him out, and that was fine by me. I'd had enough after four days of trying to push him out the normal way.

"Where's the baby?" I said when I woke up, panicking and looking down at my stomach.

"Here he is," said Pete, gently putting my tiny bundle of baby boy in my arms.

With my second pregnancy, I decided to stay awake to watch my baby being born. Planned to the minute in the controlled environment, I knew when it was happening and wanted to be awake this time.

The incision didn't feel anything like how it looked to the obstetrician who had to cut through my stomach muscles and uterus wall to get to the baby. At my end, it felt like nothing more than someone tugging on a belt loop, had I been wearing a pair of jeans. I concentrated on my excitement at meeting my next child for the first time and tried not to think about what else was going on involving scalpel knives and clamps.

"Holy shit, I can see your insides," Pete said.

"Cheers for that, Pete," I said, as I put my head to the side and puked up one final time.

"No, honestly I can, your intestines and everything. It's sick," Pete said, staring down at what the doctor's hands were doing.

"Pete?"

"Yeah?" Pete said without looking up.

"Fuck off."

"Oops, yeah, sorry. Not helpful."

"Not really."

The doctor, smiling behind his surgical mask, said to Pete, "Why don't you stand at the top end by Sarah's head? Then you can both see the baby as it arrives."

"Good idea," Pete said, shifting himself promptly.

"Are you ready?" the doctor asked.

"Yes," I replied.

The doctor scooped my baby out of my body.

"Here she is," he said. "And she is beautiful."

I thought I was the cleverest person, ever. As if having a boy then a girl had never happened to anyone before in the history of the universe.

The row of medical students at the bottom of the operating table thought I was clever too.

"Of course they can watch," I'd said when asked.

They clapped, shook each other's hands, patted each other on the back as if one of them had just given birth and tearfully gave their thanks for letting them see my daughter being born.

My girl entered the world to a standing ovation.

11

Six-week time frames held significance in my new life because these were the intervals between the blood tests I now had to have. What happened in the first six-week period would largely remain a blur and difficult to recall with much clarity.

I tried not to think about what would happen to me if the treatment didn't work, silently obsessing over taking the tablets Alex had given me, fearful I would somehow forget to take one. I wanted only for the day to be over, get back into bed again and slip into unconsciousness. This thought was the only one that soothed me.

I must have tried to function as best I could. I still went to work and looked after my children at the very least. Robin cooked and fed us a lot which was kind of him, not that I took much notice of his thoughtfulness. When he tried to coax me into being the old me by sharing a funny story or joking around with false jolliness, I would stare at him coldly while reminding him that was over now, that person was gone.

I tried to behave like my old self on the very few occasions I had to leave the house other than to go to work. Conveniently, Robin's presence provided a smoke screen. People I knew thought I was simply having the best of times with my new beau and too loved-up to bother with other company.

On one of these occasions, bare cupboards making a weekly food shop a necessity, I inescapably ran into someone I knew at the supermarket. As if it wasn't going to happen. Make-up Lynn, made-up to the hilt. She commented happily that I looked slim and tired, her lip-lined peaks pointing at her nostrils as she spoke. She used her observations on my appearance to guide the way to a conversation about Robin.

"Is that fabulous French boyfriend of yours keeping you up at night and wearing you out?" She said.

"Well…" I muttered.

"Don't be shy, darling, how did you manage that? Young, handsome and a Frenchman to boot! Just outstanding. I wish I could pull it off," Make-up Lynn said as she nudged me with her elbow, her bronzer glowing under the florescent lighting of Morrisons marketplace as shiny as the kippers in her hand basket.

"Robin is Robin, what can I say?" I said, shrugging my shoulders non-committedly and smiling ventriloquist dummy widely and uncomfortably.

"You lucky, lucky girl. Enjoy!" Make-up Lynn said in a growly kind of eat-men-for-breakfast voice, as she swanned off in the direction of the pre-packed salads.

I didn't feel very lucky. However, this provocative notion made keeping up appearances easier and did its job well because the reality couldn't have been further from the truth. No one knew or suspected I wasn't me anymore and they were talking to a doppelganger. The counterpart copy of the old me. A walking, identical double. My HIV twin.

Six weeks after the first round of blood tests I received a call from Eve. She sounded excited, eager to get the conversation underway.

"Your blood test results are back. I have good news for you, Sarah."

Good news from Eve hadn't happened before.

"Oh?" I replied. "How good?"

Eve ran out some numbers that didn't really mean anything to me.

"But you're still talking in thousands."

"What I'm telling you is the viral load in your blood is way down compared to when you were diagnosed. The HIV in your body has halved. I've never seen such a dramatic turnaround in such a short amount of time," Eve said.

"Okay, that does sound like good news. What does it mean for the future? Am I going to be alright?"

"Your CD4 cell count has risen, it's fighting back. You have an immune system again. Your body is starting to look after itself. This is what that means, Sarah. Treatment is working, and yes, I think you are going to be okay."

"Told you," the hopeful me said to the realistic me.

Six weeks on again and the next set of results would show my CD4 count was at a safe level. It was low compared to someone who did not have HIV but good enough.

The goal of achieving an undetectable viral load had been reached and Eve was delighted for me because this was the safest way to be HIV-positive. The amount of virus in my body was so small it could not be detected by the machine that analysed my blood samples in the hospital laboratory. Undetectable was a very important word to people living with HIV. It was the word that meant they were alive.

"You are still HIV-positive. The rules still apply with sexual partners. You would still test positive in a blood sample," Eve the Parole Officer said.

"Yes governor, thank you governor. Give over, Eve, I know that."

"I have to say these things. Sorry," Eve said, genuinely apologetic.

"It's okay. How come I'd still test positive if the virus isn't multiplying?" I asked.

"The small amount of remaining HIV cells in your body are sleeper cells and inactive. This is the reason why your immune system doesn't recognise them as a threat that needs to be dealt with. Your body will still be producing HIV antibodies because of them. A test would pick this up," Eve explained.

"I see," I said.

"You'll get the hang of it," Eve said. "You'll become your own little expert in HIV soon and sound like one of us."

"Great. Every girl's dream," I replied.

These sleeper cells were sneaky little bastards.

They lay dormant and hid in clever places. Reservoirs of them were still in my brain and my lymph glands. Snoozing like grizzly bears in their caves, my medication had knocked them out like a tranquilliser dart, so they couldn't do any more damage. But, and this was a big but, if I stopped taking my tablets, they would wake up, very, very annoyed.

My mood lifted, how could it not? It was the relief more than anything else. I did not feel like the old me, but I was humbled by the experience of my diagnosis and the opportunity to receive treatment, a privilege deserving people in other parts of the world did not get.

12

Robin, true to his word, stayed in England much longer than he had originally intended. I wasn't sure why anymore; so much had changed. He told me he felt responsible, guilty almost, that he was the reason I knew of my HIV status. Even when I pointed out how grateful I was that he may well have saved my life, he insisted it was still the way he felt, as irrational as it was.

Regardless of his guilt, or because of it, Robin still wanted to have a physical relationship with me, even in the early days of my diagnosis. I wanted the comfort of his company and nothing more. It wasn't a joint attempt at having more than just a friendship because unless caught off guard, I was having none of it.

I avoided any physical contact that went anywhere near comprising my plan, the part to stay celibate. I didn't understand Robin's persistence and he didn't understand my reluctance. It was impossible for him, in all his youthful, beautiful, HIV-negativeness.

Robin felt him being there and wanting to stay with me, should have been enough to put things right. I would yell at him it was not about that, because it was not about him, frustrated he could think it was so straightforward.

I found it all so wearing. I was barely coping with my own emotions, let alone someone else's. Our relationship became an overplayed cat-and-mouse game that caused all sorts of angst on both sides. I would worry any closeness between us was a move towards doing something I didn't want to do, but felt guilty at the same time, after all he had done for me. Robin looked crushed by my constant rejections which made me feel terrible. Enough to make my resolve wane.

To make amends, I would sometimes try to put on an act. As a form of compensation, for one night only, I would showcase myself as the not so *Great Pretender*. Being at my most vulnerable, these attempts at forged conformity had nowhere to go other than predestined failure. I would resent Robin for making me try to be something I wasn't anymore and get angry and upset. With him, with myself, with everything.

The very last thing I felt was sexy and that meant I didn't want to have sex, even if Robin did. Robin's answer to my diagnosis might have been to carry on as if it hadn't happened, but it wasn't mine. Every ounce of my being was consumed by the news I had been given and Robin being around me, represented all I had lost.

I didn't like being touched and was terrified of the act of sex. The mere thought of it made me feel anxious and tearful. I was frightened it would somehow kill me or I would kill Robin, that consenting to sex, would result in either my demise or transgression.

The association of sex and dying was firmly embedded in my psyche because of all I had experienced, the process of procreation and the process of ceasing to live, fused together.

I might not have been able to separate them out in my head, but at least I could avoid one of these acts. Death was a part of life in its inevitability, but sex wasn't. I didn't have to have sex ever again if I didn't want to, and that, I was certain of.

The core of me, once stable and strong, was now wafer thin. A fragile glass version of my former self that could shatter into a thousand pieces at any time, especially if handled. This was me now. Delicate, handle with care. Or better still, not at all.

I surmised Robin wanted to have a physical relationship with me as a final gallant gesture, somehow wrapped up in the guilt he had talked about regarding my diagnosis. Driven by duty, a sympathy fuck, and I didn't want his charity. It was my belief a man would never find me desirable, not now. A rock-solid conviction that could not be swayed.

I felt diseased and pitiful, stripped of something that was an integral part of being a complete woman as if my sexuality had been cut out of me. I didn't see how I could possibly be someone that another person would want. I wasn't a real woman anymore.

I intended to live out my life pretending I was still a woman when really, I was nothing more than a pretty mannequin, completely empty on the inside. I might have looked like a woman, but it was a façade. I was a fake.

I could not invest in a relationship with someone else because I had nothing left to give. My relationship with my HIV had bled me dry. I felt bereft. I was grieving for the loss of the woman I once was and wanted no part of anything that brought back painful memories of her and a longing to be that person again.

It was difficult to talk to Robin about all of this for two reasons. It was painful to say out loud and on the very odd occasion I tried to explain how I felt, Robin would look at me as if I was losing my mind, and maybe I was.

Not quite a *Yellow Wallpaper* decline of mental health, but I had my moments. HIV was the captor who had locked me away from my old life and the freedom of mind it had afforded me. The walls that held me gripped in fear weren't made of bricks and mortar, they were the thoughts in my head I found impossible to control.

Robin, thinking I would eventually come around, was only trying his best to make me feel better and reinstate a relationship he desperately wanted, with all the bells and whistles. But giving up once I had an idea in my head was not me, so no number of compliments or amount of pillow talk ever changed anything. It only ever ended in tears.

Having run out of money, patience or both, Robin finally returned to France. He promised he'd be back, as soon as he had sorted out his affairs at home. I didn't press him for a return date. I didn't like myself very much for thinking it, but when the day came around to wave him off at the airport, it was a relief.

13

The great thing about the internet was, I could have a boyfriend, without panicking about all the physical aspects of a relationship that went with it.

The long-distance relationship I shared with Robin was, in my opinion, an enormous success. Having spent so much time in England, Robin and I could easily converse in simple language. This worked well for me, chatting on about nothing complicated or important. Skype on most evenings, we talked, or sometimes just sat and watched television together like a normal couple, except there were five hundred miles between us.

Robin liked his rugby matches in France. I would choose favourite movies to watch in England. Sometimes to please him, I put French subtitles on and read the script out loud. My English accent was apparently just as appealing to the French, as it was the other way around. When we kissed goodnight, lips were puckered up and pressed on the flat plastic of our computer screens. If there was ever an opposite to a French kiss, this was it. The sentiment was there but nothing else.

Laptops next to us, we prepared Sunday lunch and ate it together. Robin in his kitchen and me in mine, across the English Channel. All perfectly safe and sanitary in my artificial romance. It reminded me of being at school as a young child. Girls would say someone in their class was their boyfriend, but he wasn't really because they never saw each other apart from in the playground. Computer screens were mine and Robin's playground. I thought it was a super way of having a relationship. Robin, being a normal person, hated it.

When it all ended abruptly, I accepted it without question. Robin had clearly found his better judgement and decided not to bother with the likes of me. After a while, I received an apologetic phone call from him. He wanted to let me know how sorry he was for his silence and explain the reason for his absence from my computer screen.

A situation had arisen on a night out with a woman, and he couldn't bear the thought of telling me, or not telling me, so had avoided both by not speaking to me at all. Robin felt ashamed of himself but I wasn't confused or even angry. It made perfect sense to me. If I was my girlfriend, I would want to find someone else too. A relationship with a real woman wasn't exactly too much to ask for and it wasn't Robin's fault I wasn't one anymore.

"You're wasted on me," I told him, but for some reason, me saying this only made him feel worse.

I put on an affronted front for a while, because that was what women were supposed to do when they'd been cheated on, but it didn't take me too long to agree to resume our video calling. I'd missed it. After all, we had a closeness, a bond. Robin was the only person at that time, who knew.

Discovering The Joy of Skype with Robin alleviated the need to worry about sex and relationships, so I had time on my hands to worry about other things. First, there were the small things. Daily routines that before my diagnosis, I hadn't given much thought to. Suddenly, the most mundane of tasks had become a minefield of opportunity for disaster to strike. Slicing onions, for example.

For all the hundreds of thousands of meals I had previously prepared for my family, not once had I ever managed to get even the smallest of nicks from a sharp kitchen knife. But now, accidentally severing a finger and infecting everyone in the room, was a real possibility.

I imagined blood spurting from the stump where my finger used to be, like silly string gone wrong. The red poison that covered aghast members of my family, dripped off them into the shiny crimson puddles they were standing in. Even the dog got a look in. Joyfully pouncing on my finger, he would run off with it, leaving bright red paw prints as he headed for the patio doors and out to the garden to find somewhere to bury it. He'd eat it later, but that bit of the scenario was okay. Canine Immunodeficiency Virus didn't exist so at least he was one member of the family I didn't have to worry about.

The scene could have been an alternative comedy sketch, *The Comic Strip Presents...*, but most people didn't find HIV very funny and even Dawn French might've had a few problems pulling this one off.

Then there were the bigger things. The business of employment, purpose, and salary. Or lack of it. I thought about what would happen if I got sick, or if people I worked with found out and didn't want me around anymore. Like most people of my age, I lived in a house with a mortgage and a staircase. In my new life, these things had to go.

I had spotted for sale a large ground-floor apartment which had a basement with plenty of space to make bedrooms and a bathroom for my pre-graduate children. It was out of town and near the beach, which was a bonus. This meant I could downsize and have no mortgage, but the absence of a staircase in the property was its best feature.

If I were to get so sick I couldn't walk anymore, I could use a wheelchair to move me around the ground-floor rooms. I wouldn't need to bother people with requests for assistance, I would be able to manage all by myself. It was a faff, but still possible to have a wash at the bathroom sink and get dressed sitting in a chair. I knew this already because I'd tried it out.

I envisaged a time when I only had my little dog for company because I was so gloomy no one came to see me anymore. At least we could sit in the alcove of the bay window and look out at the sea, me in my wheelchair, my last and only friend on my lap.

I could have a lovely time imagining my existence in the world disappearing, my head slowly sinking into the depths of the cool blue water, hair splayed out in a circle on the surface like a tragic mermaid. From the start of my new life, I had remained fond of the thought of a watery end, the cleansing of a tortured soul.

Serious about all of this, I immediately put my house on the market and offered the vendor his asking price, but the move didn't happen because someone beat me to it with a cash purchase. I was disappointed, but I also thought it was probably about time I started to talk more about how I was feeling.

Living next to the sea would have been nice, but I wasn't sure if liking the idea of drowning in it so much, was the way I should be thinking.

The problem was, I didn't know who to talk to. I didn't want to burden Robin. Aside from it not being fair, I liked our simple exchanges. I didn't want to have complex conversations with him. When I told Robin about the apartment, we didn't get much past why seagulls weren't big chickens that liked living by the sea, and he still called them sea chickens.

"Robin, I've been to look at an apartment for sale close to the beach. It would be nice to wake up to the sound of the waves, if I can hear them over the seagulls screeching, that is," I had told him, pleased with myself that I had found a solution to my potential lack of money and mobility circumstances.

Robin had been more interested in talking about seagulls rather than the reasons why I wanted to move to a new property.

"What is a seagull?" he asked.

"A big bird that lives by the sea," I replied, trying to remember if I'd ever seen a seagull in France.

"Ah, chickens of the sea."

"Not a chicken, a gull."

"Okay, if you prefer, girl of the sea. She has eggs, yes?"

"Yes, but that doesn't mean seagulls are the same as chickens."

"You sure? Can you eat them?"

"No, Robin, you can't eat a seagull."

"Why?"

"It's illegal," I replied, trying to remember if I'd ever heard of anyone getting arrested for eating a seagull.

And so, it would go on, good enough for me. I liked our conversations this way. I had a feeling Robin would not want to know about my dark thoughts. All he wanted, was for me to get better and be the old me again.

I had friends I could turn to, but when I looked at them in all their womanly beauty, the last thing I felt like doing was telling them. They wouldn't have understood because they were real women.

Sometimes I wondered what would happen if I kept bottling all my strange thoughts up. I might have just exploded one day. There were times when I wanted to loudly vocalise, with a heavy emphasis on the use of obscenities, how I felt about HIV.

Round about the same time as the beach apartment move, that didn't happen because of the flashy cash purchase person, I was made to attend a training event at work. I had to spend the entire day with a bunch of people I didn't know that well.

Not wanting to be there and not wanting to be nice to anyone, I felt annoyed and agitated at being placed in such a position by my employer. Even though, I was fully aware, an easy day in a pleasant location with lunch provided, would not usually make someone feel like a tightly wound up spring in a confined space.

During the icebreaker, we had to share something about ourselves that nobody else in the room knew and the lack of originality was staggering. There must have been over forty attendees in the room, sitting in the large circle their chairs had formed. All it took was one boring contribution and the next few people would follow suit with something similar.

People were saying stupid things like what they called their cat or that they were planning a trip to Thailand to wash elephants. Even worse, someone even had the audacity to talk about their new en-suite and how many bathrooms they now had because of it.

Pets, holidays and houses. These were the running themes.

All these people with all their trivia, I had thought. *How dare they be so fucking ordinary?*

When it came to my turn, all I wanted to do, was stand up and shout, "Big fucking deal! I am HIV-positive! Is that all you lucky bastards have got to think about? Your next holiday or how many places in your house you can take a crap? Give me a fucking break.

One of you morons will be wanking off to a brochure on grape picking in the Dordogne next."

Maybe I should have, it might have made me feel better. But I didn't, because then I would have had to quit my job, making me unemployed with a not very helpful reference recommending I considered an anger management programme.

Rather than risking an outburst I would later regret, I decided to go and see Eve. My visits to the clinic were only necessary every three months by this time. The only reason I went was for my usual blood test and to pick up more medication. Eve had always made it explicit, I could go and see her anytime if I wanted to talk, and I was ready to take her up on her offer.

Eve wasn't HIV-positive, I had already asked her that. She had been faithfully married to a physics lecturer for thirty-five years but had once taken a rapid HIV test to see just how rapid, rapid was, out of curiosity. Her test had come back negative, but she had a lot of experience supporting people whose tests came back positive.

I found some comfort in that at least, because most of the time, I felt like the only person on the planet living with HIV was me.

14

Conversations with Eve became a regular thing. Other people popped out to the bingo in their spare time, I liked to visit a sexual health clinic and talk about dying.

It had occurred to me, if the CD4 cells in my immune system continued to do their job and fight off infection and diseases in the way they were supposed to, then presumably there was no hurry to purchase a wheelchair or go down to the Co-op and sort out a funeral plan. This was good, but there was a flip side to it. It also meant I had to put up with living as an HIV-positive person and this posed the question to myself, what if I couldn't do that?

It wasn't so much I was suicidal, I didn't label it or overcomplicate it, I simply enjoyed thinking about how great it would be for everything to just stop. Like a fairground attendant pulling the brakes on his waltzer carriages until the touching metal surfaces brought the ride to a halt.

I hadn't wanted those treats at the fair to end as a kid. The spinning and the music, lost in the rush of giddy excitement for those few moments of pleasure, until it was someone else's turn to step inside the carriage.

Now, I wondered what would happen if there came a time, I wanted off the ride before it came to an end.

HIV was such a buzzkill.

These thoughts led me to be interested in how long it would take to die if I stopped taking my tablets, so I asked Eve about it. I was aware this would come across controversial and I didn't mean to sound ungrateful, but it seemed like the obvious question to ask for someone in my position and I wanted to have a discussion about it.

It wasn't that I intended to refuse medication, not until a time when it became completely necessary, anyway. What I wanted was to still feel in control of me and thinking of it as an option afforded me this benefit. HIV believed itself to be the established authority in my body and I didn't much care for this arrangement.

After all, the virus needed a host to live in.

Checkmate.

My treatment by now consisted of only having to remember to take one combined tablet at bedtime, which wasn't difficult, but the side effects were. Nausea and tiredness, and then there were the nightmares. Not senseless and fuzzy in the way dreams usually were, mine had more of a disaster movie feel to them and I had been dropped from nowhere into the middle of an adrenaline-pumped action scene. They were crystal clear as if watching a big-screen production, only I wasn't sitting in the audience eating popcorn, I was the main headliner. I had seen myself in the middle of tornadoes, on sinking ships, jumping from burning buildings and running from tsunamis.

I had once dreamt about the apocalypse. People who couldn't get underground quick enough got saturated by polluted acid rain pouring down from the skies, the thin ropes of water a glistening pink, the colour of diluted blood.

Those who became contaminated lost the power to control their impulses and desires. People were stealing cars, frantic to get to wherever they were going to cause mayhem. Others were running around with guns shooting people. I could see women being grabbed off the street, dragged kicking and screaming through doorways, by men they usually only greeted when putting the bins out.

I had spent the entire night jumping out of the way of cars, dodging bullets and fighting off neighbours trying to kidnap me. What woke me up was my heart painfully thumping in my chest. My dreams were exhausting. Most mornings I woke up feeling like I had been fighting for my life.

Another side effect of taking medication that hadn't happened, but could, worried me a lot. It was a condition called Lipodystrophy and linked to the long-term use of antiretroviral drugs. If this were to happen to me, it would result in seriously irregular body fat displacement all over my body. I would lose fat from my face and limbs and gain it around my internal organs and abdominal area.

Worst of all, a large protuberance formed of solid fat would get bigger and bigger at the base of my neck, referred to medically as a buffalo hump. The reason being, that was exactly what it looked like.

On passing a mirror in my house, I had stopped doing the usual hairdo inspection most women couldn't resist and started poking and prodding my body, looking for signs of lumps of fat growing in strange places. I was particularly worried about ending up looking like a long-gone era carnival oddity. Elephant Man had had his day. Move over. Buffalo Lady had arrived.

Eve insisted she had never seen the condition in a patient before, probably because it was an issue with older drugs. However, I still tortured myself with images of people on the internet who had developed the condition and I knew just how debilitating it could get.

Withered, emaciated limbs and painfully extended abdomens caused restricted movement and breathing difficulties, the physical appearance of individuals completely disconnected from their former selves. The disturbing images of gaunt faces on creepy old medical photographs told a tale of suffering and reminded me of pictures I'd seen of Holocaust victims. My research into the condition left me thinking if this were to happen to me, staying alive by taking the medication that caused it, didn't make much sense.

It was the bleakness. The hopelessness of it all that got to me. There was no cure and that was that, no beacon of light in the darkness that anyone could give me. Alex had a stock answer when I asked him about it, the one he probably gave to all his patients and he didn't beat around the bush delivering it. HIV was here to stay and had to be managed just like other illnesses people learnt to live with.

Nothingness had an appeal like never before. The thought of my own death didn't trouble me anymore. On the contrary, I visualised it as a warm blanket being placed around my shoulders that I could tightly wrap myself up in. It blocked out everything, my blanket. When it shrouded me, all the worry and all the pain just slowly slipped away.

I wanted to know if stopping treatment was a viable get out clause from living with HIV, my own euthanasia plan, should I ever need it.

Eve listened patiently before speaking, her eyes filled with compassion.

"If you stop taking your medication, you will die a slow and painful death in a hospital ward. As any medical practitioner who has attended to patients with advanced HIV at the end of life would tell you, it's amongst the worst deaths they have seen. It isn't quick. One disease builds on another until the body can't cope anymore."

She reached over and took my hand and squeezed it gently.

"The only way to stop this from happening is to keep treatment going. Please. Keep on taking your tablets. You will not always feel like this, I promise."

I couldn't see how, but I hoped so.

15

A subject that often arose during my visits to the clinic, was a time in my life that came to be known and referred to as The Fog. I wasn't one for clichés, but I couldn't think of a more apt word for it, the analogy used as an abbreviation and slipping into the conversations I had with Alex and Eve.

It summarised perfectly the way I felt about the dark mist that surrounded a pivotal point in my life where I didn't know what had happened to me. The point at which my old life finished and my new life began.

I didn't know when or by whom, the hooded, silent assailant that was HIV, had entered my body and my life. I knew I had to accept this, no amount of talking would change the fact. Yet it helped to express it and have the significance of this being another loss I had to learn to live with, acknowledged by another person.

My HIV status had nothing to do with Mark, he was fine. I knew this because I had already asked Eve for reassurance he'd been in for a test. I wanted to know, Mark hadn't got a fright, ignored Eve's messages, or put letters from the clinic in the bin. Some people did, I had been surprised to hear, when Eve had once mentioned it.

"Sarah, you know the reasons why I can't tell you if Mark has been in for a test," Eve had said when I'd asked.

"Even though it was me who told you to contact him? I know what he's like for putting stuff off that he doesn't want to do, that's all," I'd replied.

"Sorry," Eve had said.

"I'm not asking you to tell me test results, I just want to make sure he came in and then I can stop thinking about it."

"Fair enough," Eve had said, slightly bristly. "All sorted. Now stop thinking about it."

Eve had managed to get in touch with Mark. I now knew that. I could tell Eve knew him by the tone of her voice. Mark had a habit of rubbing people up the wrong way if something was not to his liking and being summoned to a sexual health clinic for an HIV test, fitted into that very neatly.

Besides, Mark was still Mark. I saw him around town occasionally in new cars, new clothes, with new girls. It was pretty obvious that Mark had not been told by Eve he was HIV-positive.

Where I came from exes often remained on friendly terms. Not that we were a polygamous society or anything like that, it was more of a 'no hard feelings' attitude amongst couples who were mature enough to see their match was not one made in heaven and going nowhere. In a small town, it made life easier to be pleasant, so that's what most people were.

The other men in my previous life were not difficult to contact because of the amicability that existed in my town. It was what to say once I had, that was the hard part.

James, didn't know the reason why we hadn't worked out was because of his predecessor, Gorgeous Gary. However, my lingering feelings for another hadn't stopped us from becoming close at one time. He had met my family and for this reason if nothing else, I thought he would be considerate of my feelings when I told him the reason why I wanted him to go for an HIV test.

We arranged to meet up but when I saw him, my nerve went and I couldn't do it. I couldn't tell James the real reason for my visit. He was too pleased to see me, eager to know why his ex-girlfriend had shown up. I struggled with being the bearer of bad news at the best of times and the conversation I'd intended to have with him, I found impossible.

James was the proud owner of a posh bathroom shop, so instead of saying it would be a good idea for him to go for an HIV test, I asked him questions about plumbing. Specifically, how to install a bathroom into a basement. I wasn't buying the apartment next to the beach anymore, that ship had sailed, but I couldn't think of anything else to say when caught on the hop and James liked talking about bathrooms.

After a long conversation about u-bends, hot and cold water pipe installation, and drainage solutions in below ground level property, I left James scratching his head over why a discussion about it all had been so urgent.

"I didn't know you had a basement," he said, as I got in my car.

"I don't. It was a project. It's complicated," I said as I drove off, waving goodbye out of the car window, desperate to get away.

When I told Eve about it, although amused by my description of the intense meeting about the importance of waste in a waste pipe flowing in the right direction, it took a fair amount of restraint for her not to say, "I told you so."

What she did say made total sense. As Eve was the person who performed the HIV tests on people identified through partner notification, she was well rehearsed in handling the situation because she had completed quite a few.

"People come to the clinic angry, I'm not denying that, but when I point out their name was given out of concern for their safety, because no one actually has to do it, the majority get it and calm down. I can't force anyone to discuss their relationships with me," Eve told me.

"What if they don't get it and don't calm down?" I asked.

"I quite enjoy telling indignant individuals that it can't be ruled out, they might be the person in the relationship the virus originated from. That sharp shuts them up."

"And if their test comes back negative?"

"When test results come back negative, which the majority do, it's a lesson learnt. They've had a moment, no matter how fleeting, of having to consider the possibility they are about to learn they are HIV-positive. For most, that is quite an enlightening experience."

"What about the ones who aren't enlightened?"

"I tell them they are lucky. Not only to have escaped the virus, but also because someone cares enough about them to have handed over their details to us. I ask them to be kind because unlike the passing distress they've experienced, the person who provided their name faces a lifetime of being HIV-positive. I ask them, if they think they know who that person is, to keep it to themselves."

"That makes sense," I said to Eve. "It would convince me."

"I like to think it would most people," Eve said. "It isn't much to ask, of anyone with a conscience anyway."

Eve knew what she was doing, there was no doubt in my mind about that. I had spent enough time with her to know how convincing she could be. Eve was firm but fair. I had faith in her 'keep your trap shut down the pub' talk because if she told me not to do something, I wouldn't do it. Eve had a Head Teacher type quality about her which was a necessary attribute given what she did for a living. A shrinking violet she was not.

After meeting with James, I knew it was the right decision to leave it in Eve's very capable hands and with huge relief, I found out at a much later date, no one Eve contacted tested positive.

Thankfully this was not, after all, an item on my list of horrors I had needed to worry about.

16

There came a time when Eve didn't want to talk about The Fog anymore. She preferred our conversations to centre around a much more cheerful subject, how well I looked and how far I had come, a year on from my diagnosis.

I liked it when she said such reassuring things, but this didn't mean I was prepared to forget about The Fog as if it wasn't important to me anymore. Talking about it kept the subject alive. The truth of the matter was, I wanted answers. I wanted to put together all the pieces of my new life, so I could step back from it and see the whole picture.

This was difficult for Eve, she had to be careful what she said because of patient confidentiality. I didn't mean to make it awkward for her. I could see she mentally screened the content of our conversations before she spoke, and because of this, I tried to be as tactful as I could when we talked.

Eve could have been blunt, she could have told me to belt up, but she didn't. She wanted me to feel better and move on with my life so badly. If I got on her nerves repeating myself, she was decent enough not to show it. Mostly, Eve would try to guide the dialogue between us in a different direction and I understood why.

If I was never going to know the details of how I came to be

HIV-positive, then there was little to achieve from going over it any more than we had already. Her advice was, I should settle myself, leave it be and concentrate on the future.

"I know of people who tested positive at the same time as their current, or a previous partner. Usually, in such a situation, there is no way of determining within any degree of accuracy, who had the virus first. It is best for you to accept this is just the way of it, however hard that might be," Eve said, during one of our conversations.

"What if I can't accept it?" I asked.

"You have to. Mother Nature is a crafty old bird who likes to keep us guessing. Some people feel it is better not to know, particularly couples who are both positive and still together."

As sensible as her words were, it was easier said than done.

I tried, but I couldn't convince myself to feel the same way. The not knowing, overrode it. For me, it was as if my life had taken a sharp turn in the wrong direction from its intended course. I told myself everyone diagnosed with HIV felt this way, as if something had gone terribly wrong, but it didn't help. Inexplicably, I felt there was something I should know, that I didn't.

I described these feelings to Eve on a visit to the clinic to pick up my next prescription. I wasn't expecting anyone, including Eve, to come up with any answers. However, I could never quite resist the temptation to bring it up whenever she asked me how I was feeling.

I expected Eve to do her usual turnabout on the subject and change it to something with a feel-good factor. Her favourite was my skin. It gave Eve genuine pleasure to talk about how well I looked, compared to when she had first met me.

Once on treatment, my skin issues had cleared up and my hair grew back thick and shiny. I was HIV-positive and positively glowing in good health. It amused me when people commented on it. I got asked what my secret was because they wanted whatever I had.

On this occasion, Eve's response was different.

"I've thought of something that might help," she said.

I got the feeling it was more of a gesture, a demonstration of support rather than something Eve believed would provide me with the resolution I craved. However, she must have thought it was worth giving it a go. If for no other reason than to prove to me once and for all, how futile my persistence with the subject was.

Eve asked if I could recall having an illness over the last few years, memorable due to the intensity of feeling unusually sick with symptoms similar to flu. Lingering fatigue after the illness would have been another indicator that this was not the usual type of flu people got in the winter months.

As soon as Eve said it, I remembered an illness that matched her description. A sudden, long-forgotten memory of the awfulness of it.

"Yes, I had that one year. I've never been so ill," I replied to Eve's question.

Eve leant forward when she next spoke. "Really? That's interesting."

"I called the doctor out because I was so concerned with what could be wrong with me. It's the only time in my life I've ever done that."

Eve went on to talk about something I hadn't heard of before and as I listened, The Fog began to lift.

"There's a condition when a person first becomes HIV-positive. A reaction is the best way to describe it, one that makes some people feel extremely ill. Want to hear more? I don't want to bombard you with the science stuff," Eve asked.

I wasn't usually that interested in the science stuff but this conversation was different.

"Yes," I replied eagerly. "Please, continue."

"It's called seroconversion, as in something converting, an event that brings about a change. In this context a person converting from HIV-negative to positive. Once the virus has entered the body, the immune system fights to protect itself by producing HIV antibodies and it is this that causes the flu-like symptoms. Not everyone experiences it but those who do describe it as the worst flu they've ever had, or so they'd thought at the time."

"The usual flu symptoms? Nothing else out of the ordinary?" I asked.

"The usual ones associated with flu but way more severe. Less common but more suggestive of HIV infection is a rash. Usually around the middle area but in more extreme cases it can spread down the limbs too. I have also heard people describe seroconversion as a physically painful experience and when you think about the war that was raging inside their body at the time, that doesn't come as a surprise."

Eve broke off from her explanation and asked, "Is that helpful? Does any of it sound familiar to you?"

"Yes, it does," I replied.

"How much of it?" Eve asked, intrigued.

"All of it," I answered.

I distinctly remembered being that sick because I was rarely unwell. I had taken time off work and stayed in bed for two whole weeks. I felt so terrible I couldn't make it to the surgery and when the doctor knocked on my front door, I remembered worrying she would turn around and get back in her car because it took me so long to get down the stairs to let her in.

Everywhere hurt. The pain throughout my entire body made every muscle and joint ache. I could barely stand up because my legs struggled to keep me upright, I had to keep the blinds down on the windows because daylight stung my eyes with a burning heat and my head pounded as if a small explosion had gone off in it.

Since the usual childhood illnesses, I had caught the odd bug but nothing compared to this. It felt as if a poison was coursing through my veins, reaching every part of my body. I remembered standing in front of the full-length mirror in my bedroom, clutching its frame with one hand for support and undoing the belt on my dressing gown with the other. I was taken aback at the splotchy pink rash covering the whole of my body that had developed overnight. I had guessed at glandular fever or an adult strain of measles because I couldn't think what else it could possibly be.

The illness had stood out alright, there was no mistaking that.

"When was it?" Eve asked.

"I don't know," I replied, brow furrowed as I thought about it.

"Roughly?"

"No idea. If I guess, I could be miles out. It was a while ago now, I'm going to have to think about it."

I couldn't for the life of me remember when I'd had the illness. I couldn't pinpoint a date. I couldn't even narrow it down to a year. The only thing that kept on resonating in my head, was that I'd been worried enough to call out the doctor.

17

The penny had dropped, I'd called out the doctor.

That meant, I was on the brink of possibility.

Now I knew about seroconversion, the missing pieces of my new life were potentially available to me. All I needed to do was figure out when my body had been fighting off, albeit unsuccessfully, HIV.

I could have called the doctors' surgery and arranged an appointment to ask for the date from my medical records, but that seemed like a lot of unnecessary explaining. Physicians in regular practices didn't see a lot of HIV. Had they ever attended to someone seroconverting, in all likelihood the person's symptoms would have been given a way less complicated diagnosis, leaving the virus unrecognised and undetected.

I believed this had happened to me. Yet still, that didn't make the thought of explaining all of this to an over-worked GP who only wanted to get home in time to put his kids to bed and didn't know what the bloody hell I was talking about, anything other than off-putting.

I was at work, everyone had left and I was alone. I had waited for the last person to leave on purpose, and now, the filing cabinet in front of me had my full attention. I was wondering whether one of the drawers I was looking at held the missing piece, to the puzzle that was my new life.

During the day, I'd thought about the doctor's house visit a lot. It was strange how I could remember the conversation I'd had with her but couldn't pull into my conscious awareness any other peripheral features about my personal circumstances at the time.

I knew the house I was living in because I could picture it, even small details like the colour of the blinds in my bedroom. The only other aspect of the day that I remembered, was calling my manager and telling her about the rash. The same manager I had now, which meant, I was in the same room as my sickness absence record.

I was methodical and organised at work, I liked order. I couldn't remember doing it, but was almost sure I would have kept a copy of the doctor's sick note in my personnel file. I walked over to the filing cabinet and with a few quick fingertip flicks, found what I was looking for. I reminded myself to breathe when I read what I had needed to know for so long. The date on the sick note told me when and how I came to be HIV-positive.

Like a switch being turned on in my head, a memory fired up, sharp and clear as if I was watching it on a high-definition screen. It sent a shiver through me; a ghost from the past had returned.

I was lying in bed after the doctor had left when I heard the front door open. It was my partner at that time, coming in from work. He walked up the stairs and looked around the door to check I was awake before entering the room and starting a conversation.

"Feeling any better?" he asked.

"Not really," I replied, "I was worried, so I called the doctor. She's been out to see me. It isn't measles or glandular fever. She doesn't know what it is, so there's no point in taking antibiotics."

"Oh?"

"I've caught a virus off someone. A strange, unusual virus. That's all she's written on the sick note to send into work."

There was no reaction from him after that. The idea of the doctor's visit and staying in the insalubrious environment my virus was causing, seemed to have alarmed him. Off like a shot, he said nothing more and walked out of the room.

Well, so much for tea and sympathy, I had thought indignantly.

It took a while to recover and bounce back to what I thought was my normal self, after the illness. What was never the same again, was my relationship with Mark.

18

Robin was coming over to England for my birthday. I was looking forward to seeing him in 3D, it would make a pleasant change from my usual preference of boyfriend, the flat-screened type. Just before setting off to collect him from the airport, Eve called.

"Can you call in to see us tomorrow? Nothing to worry about, we have something we would like to talk to you about that will interest you."

She sounded relaxed and cheerful, delighted to hear Robin was back for a visit. I couldn't persuade Eve to divulge any further information on the phone, so gave up and told her I would see her in the morning.

I entertained myself with the thought Alex and Eve had planned a surprise birthday party at the clinic for me, as I picked up my car keys and walked out the front door. I pictured all the nurses in their disposable white aprons and blue vinyl examination gloves, standing quietly behind the electric doors waiting for me, party horns and blowouts at the ready.

"Surprise! You are HIV-positive! Hip-Hip, Hooray!" they would shout, hanging on to their little pointy triangle hats to stop them falling off in the excitement of my arrival. Thread elastic was never enough to keep those darned things in place.

The morning after Eve's call, I left Robin sleeping and made my way to the clinic early, keen to press on with our day once I had found out what Eve wanted to talk about. It couldn't be anything important. The worst news anyone could receive from a sexual health clinic had already happened, way back.

The receptionist at the clinic asked me to take a seat in the waiting room and almost instantly Eve appeared at one of the doorways leading off from it. She waved and beckoned me to follow her and as we walked down the corridor, Eve told me she had booked one of the little meeting rooms for us to talk in.

Once in it, Eve said she wouldn't be long and went off to find Alex. I was accustomed to all the spaces in the building by now, I had been in most of them at one time or another. At ease with the place, I fiddled with things on the table to the side of the sofa I was sitting on, then wandered around the room to read the posters on the walls about STIs to pass the time.

I started to feel curious; I wasn't usually put in a room on my own and asked to wait. Today was different from other days. We weren't in Alex's clinical room so I knew the meeting wasn't about my health, otherwise, he would have wanted to take some more of my blood to look at. Other than to hear bad news, I hadn't been asked to come to the clinic in between appointments before.

When Eve and Alex walked in, I felt the usual warmth and affection I had for both of them. After all, they knew more about me than my parents did. They looked after me, they were my new life Ma and Pa.

Over time, I had slowly started to recover, just as Eve had promised I would. Not that my diagnosis and the shock of the reality of my situation hadn't taken its toll. The immediate and prolonged trauma had been punishing. I had come across an article in a magazine once on women and Post-Traumatic Stress Disorder and had recognised myself in the text.

I had experienced a life-threatening trauma. It was linked to sex and I had feelings and thoughts of being assaulted even though I didn't know why. I had been injured. I'd had a severe reaction to the event, my diagnosis, and I more than refused support from people I knew. I didn't tell anyone what had happened to me and actively pushed people away. I deliberately and purposefully isolated myself.

As I read through the article, gripped by its content, I had mentally ticked every single familiar item on the symptoms list.

Depression. Tick.

Relentless worrying. Tick.

Intense guilt. Tick.

Emotional numbness. Tick.

Anhedonia. Tick.

The nightmares when I was asleep were bad enough, but the irritability and irrational thoughts when fully awake had been the real scary monsters that lived under the bed, in the months following my diagnosis.

Alex and Eve each pulled up a chair to be closer to where I was sitting, positioning themselves directly in front of me. I started to wonder if I had done something wrong and upset them. Alex looked unusually and disconcertingly uncomfortable.

When he started talking about The Fog, I listened only to be polite. I didn't understand why we needed to go over it again. Alex and Eve knew all about the doctor's sick note I had found in my filing cabinet at work and what it represented. They knew it was over for me and I didn't need to think about it anymore. The Fog had gone.

"You've talked about The Fog a lot when you've come to the clinic. It's very important to you, isn't it?" Alex asked.

"It was, but I've got my answers now. I consider myself very lucky, to have had the means to find out, how my life has come to be what it is," I answered, still unsure why we were talking about it.

To my surprise, tears welled up in Alex's eyes when he next spoke.

"I have something to tell you. All we want is for you to be happy," he said.

"I know that, Alex, and I'm trying, I really am. It's better now, than before."

"To be happy and lead a full life. Not a partial existence because you don't know what happened to you," Alex continued.

"I do know what happened to me," I said, still confused.

"What really happened to you. I wasn't sure for a long time and thought it better that you didn't know, but I have come to believe you have the right to know the truth."

Alex leant forward in his chair and put his hands together before speaking again.

"I sincerely hope I have made the right decision. This is to help you move on and your persistent talk about The Fog made my mind up. What I need you to understand, is that we are doing this for you. No other reason. Your reaction to your diagnosis was difficult to witness, we were very worried about you and all we want, is the best for you."

Eyes like saucers, I turned to Eve. She was reading from a sheet of paper, a script, prepared in advance for our meeting.

"With much moral, legal and professional debate and consideration, permission from the relevant authorities has been given to inform you of this. You have been in a relationship with someone who is HIV-positive."

Is that it? I thought.

It felt like I had opened a present on Christmas morning just to find it was something I already had. I knew I'd been in a relationship with someone who was HIV-positive because I also knew these things.

I wasn't born with HIV and didn't get it from virulent breast milk because I knew my mother wasn't HIV-positive. I wasn't a drug user who had shared a contaminated needle. I had never been in an accident or been a haemophiliac, had dialysis for renal failure, or needed a blood transfusion for any other reason and received infected blood.

I knew all these things and I also knew I got the virus from Mark and that wasn't his fault because, during the time of our relationship, he hadn't known he was HIV-positive.

I defended him. Not dissimilar to feelings of guilt, I felt a responsibility in being the instigator of someone's HIV test that had resulted in a positive diagnosis. Robin had felt the same way following mine. Mark's bad news had come about because of me and I couldn't understand why we needed to have a meeting to talk about it.

"I think it's admirable Mark is handling it so well and getting on with his life. He must have more backbone than me because all I did was cry for the first year. This is nobody's fault. Sometimes in life bad things just happen," I said to Eve.

I didn't feel any anger towards Mark. I didn't believe there was any reason why I should.

Eve waited until I had stopped talking before she tried again.

"Sarah, listen, please. Carefully this time. I need your full attention."

Speaking clearly and slowly, Eve repeated the original statement plus the last sentence I hadn't heard the first-time round, the sentence that changed everything.

"You have been in a relationship with a person who is HIV-positive," Eve said again, then looked up from her notes and directly at me. "This person knew of their status before they met you."

Not only had Eve needed permission to be able to give me this information, its delivery had to be done properly or not at all. Eve had been told to be very careful what she said to me at the clinic, while the people who knew my truth, worked out what to do about it.

Withholding what they knew from me had become intolerable for Alex and Eve. Eve had found the shame and guilt I felt, over the possibility I had put Mark at risk, particularly difficult to deal with.

When I'd told Eve about my relationship with Mark, she knew straight away what had happened to me because she already knew of him. She hadn't really needed to write down his contact details and all the other information I had given her to make sure she found him. Mark was already in the system as an HIV patient receiving treatment at a different clinic.

No personal details or dates were mentioned that would identify any one person from Alex or Eve, that wasn't allowed, but all three of us knew exactly who we were talking about. All the time I had been fighting to regain control over my physical and mental health, unknown to me another struggle had been taking place involving professional ethics.

The room remained quiet for a while. Eve and Alex were probably waiting for the usual crying to start. It didn't.

Alex and Eve kept watching me, waiting for a reaction, giving me time to grasp what I had been told. Eve eventually broke the silence and spoke first, still watching my face for a sign I understood what she had said.

"We think you've been lied to enough and we weren't prepared to contribute to that any longer. We've had to wait, but also the time had to be right for you. You were so vulnerable."

Eve handed me a piece of paper with a name and phone number written on it.

"It has to be your decision what you do next, we can't make it for you."

I looked down at it in my hand and up again at Eve as she continued talking.

"It's the number to call if you decide you want to talk to the police. An officer is on standby to take your call but it's just a precautionary measure. Take some time to think about what you want to do. You must feel upset and confused. Torn, even."

I was none of these things.

"Can I ask a question?" I said to Eve.

"Of course. We are here to help," she replied.

I picked up the receiver from the phone on the table next to me.

"What number do I press for an outside line?"

I listened to what the police officer had to say, told him I would be in touch and put the receiver down. Alex and Eve looked at each other, then back at me at the same time, as I stood up and put my coat on.

"Thank you," I said, as I hugged them both and left.

There was someone I wanted to talk to.

19

A question I was asked during the trial was if Mark had ever been abusive or controlling towards me. I told the jury the truth, that Mark had never openly been either of those things, but that didn't mean he wasn't an abuser. He was deceptive and had abused my trust. The level of his deception had come close to ending my life.

The question I asked myself, was why I agreed to see him again when it didn't feel right in the first place. Intuition, instinct, gut reaction, whatever it was that made a first impression count, I wished I hadn't ignored mine when I met Mark.

His value system wasn't the same as mine, he had a materialistic outlook on life. He liked things, not people. He parked his expensive car in spaces reserved for disabled drivers to reduce the risk of getting a scratch on it, without a hint of embarrassment or pang of conscience in doing so.

I couldn't bear pretentious behaviour in people but to my better judgement, I did see him again, fascinated at how different our worlds were. When I was with Mark, it didn't feel real and perhaps that was why I found it so exciting. I was Cinderella going to the ball before I went back to doing all the stuff I had to do in my regular life.

Mark's attentiveness towards me kept the momentum going from the start, he made me feel special. He put thought and effort into planning everywhere we went and everything we did. I had never experienced anything like it, and it worked, he grew on me. His intention from the very beginning.

I met Mark on a weekend night out, introduced to him by a friend in the group I was with. I was preparing for a charity run and the evening revolved around collecting as many sponsors as possible. My opener to getting another signature and donation was to ask Mark if he was having an enjoyable evening accompanied by a beamer of a smile.

"All the better for seeing you," was his reply, kissing me on the cheek with the confidence of an expert in the field of the fairer sex.

Mark whipped the pen and paper out of my hand and enjoying himself showing off, he wrote his name, a generous figure, and his telephone number on the sponsor form. "Call me when you have finished your run, or just call me anyway," he said.

I had no intention of calling anyone, but I did see Mark again because I kept on bumping into him. It was summertime, the weather was warm and people were outdoors making the most of the sunshine and the light nights. Sometimes when out running one of my usual routes, Mark would drive past me, circling around the streets to pass me again and shout out a flirtatious comment from the car window.

"Looking good, Sarah! Keep those knees up and call me!"

I didn't like or want uninvited attention from males in their cars when I ran, it really pissed me off, but I didn't mind when I looked up and saw it was Mark.

Another weekend into the summer months, I was in the same place as our first encounter, minus my sponsor form. Pushing my way through the crowds of noisy, cheerful people meeting up with friends, I didn't notice Mark until he grasped a hold of my hand to stop me from walking past him.

When I turned to see who had stopped me, he smiled and asked, "Let me take you out next weekend. Please."

Mark lifted the hand he was still holding and kissed the back of it softly. The charm of this action and the sincerity in his voice made me warm to him. *What could be the harm in it?* I thought as I told him where to collect me from the following Saturday evening.

We went to some very nice places that night, places someone takes you to when they are out to impress. By the end of the evening, Mark was already making plans for another date. I wasn't sure, but having had such a lovely time, I decided to go along with it.

We saw more and more of each other, and each time we did, I looked forward to the next time with increasing eagerness. I started to relax into the lifestyle Mark was so keen to give me.

Mark liked telling me how important I was to him. "I love, worship and adore you," he would say, punctuating each sentiment with a kiss. "And I am going to tell you so every day, because I want you to believe me."

I didn't need any convincing. I believed him. He was very believable. At the time, he looked like he meant every word.

My feelings for Mark and our relationship became more serious; a holiday in the south of France he took me on, made sure of that. Lying on a picnic blanket next to a lake in the mountains, Mark whispered in my ear, "Stay with me and I will look after you and treasure you for the rest of your life."

It was idyllic, all of it. The surroundings and what he was suggesting.

When Mark proposed, he must have decided well in advance it

would be abroad in a romantic setting. I didn't know he had hidden a beautiful diamond ring in his suitcase, as we set off for another holiday.

I guessed he had some sort of surprise planned when his luggage was routinely opened at passport control and his concern was disproportionate. Mark hurriedly said something to the airport official when he thought I wasn't looking and the two men gave each other a secretive little nod. I pretended not to notice, not wanting to spoil the surprise for him because I had a feeling, I knew what it was.

When Mark dropped to one knee at our clifftop apartment and asked me to marry him holding up the carefully hidden engagement ring, without any hesitation, I accepted his proposal.

I thought I was the lucky one to have him.

Mark considered the holiday a turning point in his life in two ways. The end of grieving after the death of his elderly parents and the start of a new chapter, a family of his own. An ending and a beginning of high significance.

Back at home, we started making plans for the wedding, throwing ideas back and forth about how to make it an occasion everyone would remember. We had an enviable lifestyle, full of good things.

Then I got my strange, flu-like virus and visit from the doctor.

Then all the good things stopped.

I could not figure out what had changed. Almost overnight Mark could barely look me in the eye. He became sullen and withdrawn, avoiding any physical contact with me. It got so bad if I happened to brush up against him accidentally, he would jump away from me as if it was an unpleasant experience. Mark was acting so strangely, I felt offended, and couldn't stop myself from making nippy remarks.

"God, Mark, what's wrong with you? You'd think I had an infectious disease or something," was a firm favourite.

Mark claimed the reason for his sudden quietness and distant manner towards me was his bereavement. I found this explanation hard to understand because it was out of sequence. Unhappy people did not go to the lengths Mark had, the planning to ensure he received the desired answer to his marriage proposal. I hadn't been in any hurry, Mark was the one who had pushed for commitment.

In time, I formed my own opinion for the reason why Mark's attitude towards me had changed so much.

I believed he knew what he had done.

20

The issue. Mark meets Woman and likes Woman, a lot. He doesn't want Woman or anybody else, to know he is HIV-positive.

Possible outcomes and risk index.

Pluck up the courage. Tell Woman. Live happily ever after. Unpredictable. High risk.

Pluck up the courage. Tell Woman. Woman ends relationship. Suck it up. Unsatisfactory. High risk.

Eventually tell Woman. Woman HIV-positive. Woman feels trapped. Hates Mark. Unsatisfactory. High risk.

Eventually tell Woman. Woman HIV-positive. Woman forgives Mark. Live happily ever after. Unpredictable. High risk.

Eventually tell Woman. Woman HIV-positive. Woman goes to police. Very unsatisfactory. High risk.

Never tell Woman. Secretly but safely be responsible with medication. Woman remains HIV-negative. Unrealistic. Medium risk.

Never tell Woman. Be irresponsible with medication. Woman has necessary mutated gene to be immune to HIV. Woman remains HIV-negative. Unrealistic. Medium risk.

Never tell Woman. Woman HIV-positive and put on treatment.

Lie to Woman and tell her she infected him. Stay with Woman. Woman can't believe her luck. Live happily ever after. Very satisfactory. Low risk.

Never tell Woman. Woman HIV-positive. Woman not put on treatment quick enough. Woman dies. Secret safe. Replace Woman. Satisfactory. Low risk.

21

There was no other explanation for it. Mark knew what was happening to me. I was seroconverting and about to become HIV-positive.

The immediate change in his behaviour and our relationship, everything about us as a couple that was never the same again, after the doctor's visit. Most people wouldn't have known what seroconversion was, there would be no reason for them to know. However, HIV patients did, and Mark was one.

The sick note sent to my employer and held on record. The entry into my medical record on the database at the surgery describing symptoms that sounded a whole lot like seroconversion. The doctor would have recorded her findings after visiting me. This must have worried Mark a lot and that was exactly how he looked. As if all of a sudden it had become real, the bubble that was his fantasy land had just popped.

It was as if the enormity of the situation had struck him because of evidence that could not be ignored. It became increasingly distressing for Mark to cope with what he knew as time went on. His depression was evident, and the more demanding my requests for a reason for it became, the worse it got.

Working with outcomes interested me. A starting point would

have been necessary to measure how successful Mark's desired outcome had been and I didn't have one because I didn't know what Mark was thinking when he met me. Therefore, in the absence of any assistance from Mark, who was never going to tell me the truth, I had to come up with my own answers to the burning question of motive.

Why had Mark let it happen?

There may have been some villainous master plan all along for me to become HIV-positive, a plan that included Mark not having to fess up and disclose anything he didn't want to. If it was premeditated, there were some things that Mark had not factored in. He couldn't have, they were all out of the ordinary, no one would have seen them coming.

His partner experiencing seroconversion, having it officially documented and therefore able to medically pinpoint the date of HIV transmission was one.

The decision from the health authorities, to tell me I had been in a relationship with an individual who knew he had put me at risk of HIV, was another. This wasn't just an unusual occurrence, it was a one-off. It had never happened before.

Meeting someone with a particularly persistent nature was not a plus, if the intention was to infect me and expect no resistance. I wasn't a push-over. I questioned things. Once interested in something, I had an intensity about me with no let-up. My desire for an answer to a conundrum had a hold on me until fulfilled. Sometimes I drove myself mad, let alone other people.

This facet to my personality probably went unnoticed at first by Mark. There was no reason why the true extent of my tenacity would have been highlighted in the earlier part of our relationship, honeymoon periods being what they were.

Finally, there was also the matter of his guilt. Perhaps he had not expected to feel quite as bad as he did. I sometimes wondered if Mark putting a ring on my finger was a trade-off. That in some twisted way, marrying me, made infecting me with HIV not so bad.

My opinion on Mark's intentions had gone back and forth during the investigation, but most of the time, I was inclined to think that Mark had not actually intended to transmit the virus to me. This didn't make me feel any better, I wasn't letting him off the hook. I wasn't trying to convince myself this meant Mark was an innocent party in it all.

If my HIV status was down to neglect, the absolute absence of any regard for my safety, this was possibly even worse than if he had infected me on purpose. The thought my life could be tossed aside in such a casual manner by another person, I found quite abhorrent.

Suddenly swept up in an unexpected romance, it was perfectly possible Mark had made a conscious decision not to worry about the consequences of his actions. My well-being an afterthought to him, a risk he was prepared to take to get what he wanted. I could see how that could happen. I knew of Mark's short fallings when it came to moral character, I'd been aware of them from the very beginning.

Mark would have thought it was all beneath him. The clinic visits, the intrusive questions, being told what he could and couldn't do in his private life, all that went into being an HIV patient. Not to his liking, he had pretended he wasn't one, his inflated ego backing him up all the way.

Mark had looked and behaved like a man carrying around with him a terrible secret during the final part of our relationship, the burden of it not only affecting him emotionally but also physically. Drained of energy and tired all the time, Mark took painkillers for headaches and slept a lot. It was also a convenient way of not having to look at or talk to me.

When I found out what Mark's secret was, I was pleased it had adversely affected him. I particularly liked that he had started to make himself ill with the thought of it. No wonder those headaches thumped around his head like popcorn going off in it. It wasn't in a vengeful way, more relief, to know something was going on for him in the feelings department.

If he'd felt nothing, displayed no change in behaviour of any sort, then presumably that would have made him a sociopath.

Mark being a self-centred coward was bad enough, but at least I hadn't agreed on that clifftop, to marry a charismatic nut job.

22

In the latter part of our relationship, Mark and I as a couple had broken down completely.

He may have felt sorry for everything, the broken promises, making me feel unloved and miserable, infecting me with a life-threatening virus, and wanted to make amends. Telling me to go for an HIV test was the answer, getting a tattoo with my name on it, was not.

In the early days, Mark liked to celebrate the anniversary of the date we met. Every three months, then six months and eventually annually, I would receive something to mark the occasion.

His imagination and ability to be creative, was probably why he interested me in the beginning and made the extent of his shallowness a lot less obvious. Mark's talent in his line of work was impressive, his artwork often winning awards in his field. The anniversary gifts he gave me were sometimes pieces of his work or other beautiful things. Mark always got it right, apart from the last one.

The last gift I received from Mark was a very peculiar decision for him to make. I couldn't understand the permanent, deliberate display of erroneous loyalty and connection. I thought it ludicrous because he didn't even want me anymore.

On the very last anniversary we were together, Mark asked if I would like to see my gift. Fed up with the whole situation and him by now, I couldn't have been, or looked, less interested if I'd tried. I stood waiting, one hand sassily placed on a hip, wondering why Mark was undoing his shirt.

It can't possibly be that he wants me to do the same thing, I thought as I watched him in silence. There was something about my body that now seemingly repulsed him and he stayed away from it as if his life depended on it.

The tattoo on the left side of Mark's chest was a chubby cupid clutching a big red heart.

Bloody Nora, I thought. *"It's the tattoo out of* 'True Romance'.

Draped around the heart as part of the design, was a ribbon. On it, written in a spirally, romantic font, was my name and worse still, my children's. I couldn't guess what sort of reaction he was expecting, I hadn't been able to read him for months, but he didn't seem surprised or upset at my lack of enthusiasm for his new ink work.

"Is it real?" I asked.

"Yes," Mark replied, unfazed by my response.

"It won't come off?"

"No. I hope you like it."

"Like it? Are you out of your fucking mind?"

I looked at the tattoo, in the same way I would have a squashed frog ran over on a road that I was trying not to step on. We were on the verge of breaking up and we both knew it. I wasn't his wife and my children weren't his.

To my surprise, when Mark next spoke, it was with emotion. "I know what you are thinking, but whatever happens next between us,

I want you to know you are the closest thing I've ever had to a family of my own. Even if we don't make it and I lose you, at least I can look at this and remember what I once had."

It might have been a sham, the tattoo portraying a trophy family he could claim he had once been part of. Or, it could have been guilt. An act of creative self-harming, branding himself with my name, forever. Whatever it was, in contrast to the impression the design gave, Mark's tattoo had very little to do with unconditional love. My time spent with Mark had come with a monster of a condition. HIV.

Nothing changed after the last anniversary and I got sick of the sound of my own whining about how disappointed I was with him. He rarely said anything back, my complaints usually resulting in Mark walking away and leaving the house or taking to his bed with a headache. Mark's coldness was apparent only to me; in front of people he knew, he became a different person again. At home, the usual loneliness would resume.

"Who are you going to be today, Mr. Benn?" I would say to him sourly. "Give me a clue, because I don't know anymore."

I couldn't stand it any longer. Four months after Mark had my name permanently written over his heart, I ended the relationship.

In the early days of our separation, Mark asked if I would be prepared to be seen out together, still attend functions with him and not mention to anyone that we had broken up. Unaware I had set myself up in business as an escort service, I was hurt and offended. He seemed more concerned about his public image than letting me down.

People finding out I was sick to the back teeth of him and had ended the relationship bothered him more than losing me. I declined his offer and to make my distain at his suggestion very clear, I started dating Gary Oldman, immediately.

After Mark and I parted, he asked if he could see me on two separate occasions. He wasn't seeking a reconciliation, I knew that already, Mark had transitioned back into a bachelor lifestyle with ease and being unattached suited him.

I didn't know what he wanted. There was nothing left from our relationship that connected us, other than the virus he had given me which I was unaware of. However, Mark knew about the virus we shared and for this reason, it was possible twice, Mark was looking for an absolution and going to tell me to go for an HIV test.

Sitting in a very pleasant living room in Mark's house, I listened to him for a while, waiting for the reason why my presence had been requested. Not making much sense, Mark seemed to want validity our relationship had been real at the time.

I looked at him in astonishment as I listened to his irritating use of fanciful analogies, some nonsense about lights that burn bright, burn out faster.

He must be working his way through his old DVD collection on an evening, I thought. *I can't keep up. He fancied himself as Clarence out of* 'True Romance' *not that long ago. He thinks he's Roy out of* 'Blade Runner' *now.*

It dragged on. Mark seemed to want me to help him feel better about himself and I didn't have the patience for any more of it. Annoyed, I told him the reason why we had parted was that his lack of depth as a person had made the relationship superficial.

"You got bored. It's as simple as that. Don't do it to yourself, Mark, don't look for any other explanation. You're shallow, accept it. You, doing you, is the reason why we finished," I said with confidence, at the time thinking I knew Mark possibly better than he knew himself.

I had always been a top teller-offer. Mark didn't have much more to say after that, so I left. If this was a preamble to telling me to go for a test, I had cut it short by insulting him.

The next time Mark asked if I would meet him, I didn't want to, but there was something different about his voice and curiosity got the better of me. Preferring not to go to his house again, we met in a local park and when I arrived, he was sitting on the grass waiting for me. He briefly glanced up in my direction when I approached him, then continued staring into the distance, eyes fixed on some activity at the other end of the park.

When Mark spoke, he stated he felt troubled. He was lonely and had no one to talk to. Again, I wondered why I was there, but I was kind to him this time. Mark might have been a bit of an arse, but loneliness was a terrible thing.

Feeling sorry for him, I shuffled over from my spot on the grass to sit next to the man who had put my life at risk. I put my arm around his shoulders and told him he was a smashing bloke who in time, would meet the right woman. Or man. If that was his thing. Not that there had ever been anything to suggest Mark preferred men, it was just one of the theories I had come up with to explain why he had stopped fancying me all of a sudden.

All the nice things I could think of to say, I said, to try and lift his spirits. I was warm and compassionate, I even tried to make him laugh with one of my silly stories. The more I talked, the quieter Mark became, until he was silent. He continued staring in front of him to avoid looking at me.

I had things to do and I didn't want to sit in the park with Mark any longer than I had to. I told Mark he would be fine, to go and do some shopping or soap up his newest sports car to cheer himself up, made my apologies and left.

After or during these meetings, had it ever been Mark's intention to tell me to go for a test, he had made his final decision. Telling me the truth was an unsatisfactory outcome for him. He never contacted me again and I didn't see much of him after that.

Mark didn't ever try to restart anything between us and we never came close to getting back together, in the way lots of couples did when a significant relationship came to an end. He went on to have other girlfriends who he would stick with for a while but avoided anything serious. Mark's life seemed to be back at a point that he felt most comfortable with. Only having himself to think about, his predestined, default setting.

I ran into him every now and again. We would be cordial and chat politely, about him of course. Back to his usual self, Mark would talk about his business or a recent holiday. I would watch him walk away and wonder what on earth I had been thinking of agreeing to be his girlfriend, we were so different.

My inability to work out what Mark was thinking, hadn't changed. The only reason it interested me enough to ponder on it was, when he looked at me there was nothing there, as if our past had never happened.

Mark had more than moved on. He had removed me from his mind and conscience entirely.

23

It came in waves, the anger, and lasted a long time. It was an essential part of a very painful process and I used it to my advantage.

It drove me. Whenever I felt frightened and could feel my nerve slipping away, I made myself feel angry. I whipped up the anger I felt, into a storm of hate and fury inside me.

My anger wasn't black, it was red. Red raw. A red-raw bleeding passion. For justice.

I knew it had changed me as a person and I welcomed the change. It filled the gaping wound worthlessness had gnawed away at. It gave me the chance to fight back. It told me, I wasn't a victim.

Unfocused anger was pointless, for anyone. Mine had a focus. I was angry with the right person for the right reasons. I was angry at the right time and in the right way.

My anger did not stagnate, I let it grow inside me. I did not deny my anger, I nurtured it. I allowed myself the freedom to feel whatever I needed to feel and let it flow through me.

The hate I felt for Mark eventually burnt itself clean, but it took a while.

24

Expecting new business on hearing the tinkling of the bell and the door open, Mark walked out of the office at the back of his shop.

"Sarah," he said, in way of a greeting.

I stood in the open doorway and got straight to it.

"We need to talk," I said, staring at him coldly.

There was something about his demeanour that suggested, he had thought about this moment happening already. He was prepared.

Mark calmly asked the only other person in the building to leave, a young man who was his employee, that he referred to as the dogsbody. Standing behind the counter, Dogsbody quickly shuffled around the end of it and headed for the door, when Mark told him to take an extra-early, extra-long lunch break. Without taking my eyes off Mark, I stepped to one side to let Dogsbody out, while he nervously pulled on his jacket and left without saying a word.

Mark shut the door behind him, snapped the lock, and flipped the cutesy door sign to 'closed'. He asked me to follow him into a side room, moving us both away from the large shop windows and out of view from Saturday afternoon shoppers.

I remembered the room well, it was a space in the building he had once made into a home cinema for me and the children, playing the role of family man so convincingly. With a good glug of caustic irony, I swallowed back the nasty taste that had risen in my throat as I looked at the man in front of me and thought about the two outrageously different scenarios of past and present we shared, while standing in the very same room.

Mark offered me a seat on a small sofa, while he sat on a swivel chair next to a desk, in a position that allowed him to look down at me and keep his back to the wall. With an air of control and authority, swinging from side to side in the chair, Mark asked, "And to what do I owe this pleasure?"

I stood up and spoke in a low voice, a slow, deliberate pause between each word and clenched teeth.

"When. Were. You. Diagnosed?"

Mark didn't flinch, not even the slightest flicker of an eyelid, when he replied, "I don't know what you're talking about."

"Yes, you do."

"No, I don't. Look, Sarah, you can't just barge in here and talk to me like this. I don't know what you want, but whatever it is, I can't help you."

The arrogance, the cool, self-assured way he kept up the duplicity. I exploded. I tried to hit him. I wanted to slap him across the face, hard. I'd never hit another person before, I was too slow and he caught my wrist.

"Calm down," he said, nothing more.

If someone had walked into where I worked and taken a swipe at me, I would have been more than a little curious to know the reason for it. Mark didn't question why I'd just tried to hit him. He didn't need to, he already knew.

"Stop lying!" I shouted. "I could have died in all the time you chose to do nothing. Not even an anonymous note pushed through the door to help me. Do you know what that makes you, Mark?"

Some part of me wanted to break down and cry in front of him, in the hope of provoking a reaction. I felt like a fool. It disturbed me that I had trusted a man capable of such a level of coldness. I didn't want to believe my judgement had been so wrong. I wanted a reason that made sense to me.

For the first and only time in my life, I wanted to hear some heart-wrenching story of childhood abuse and suffering. If Mark had been damaged through years of neglect and emotional deprivation as a child, then it wasn't his fault he didn't know how to treat other people. The last shred of hope I would hear something from him that I could start to understand, withered and died as I watched him.

As far as I could tell, Mark had led a privileged life. There didn't seem to be much, that Mark wanted, he didn't get and he was unaccustomed to being inconvenienced. He inadvertently looked at the phone on the desk, as if the receiver was going to magically suck him into it like a genie in a lamp, and pop him out at the other end of the line.

The destination wouldn't have mattered, anywhere would have been better than his ex-cinema room with his HIV-positive ex-fiancé. One of his expensive holiday locations would have done nicely, greeted by a hula girl with a flower garland around her neck, holding up a piña colada in a coconut shell. "Welcome to Paradise, Mr. Mark."

Either that, or he was thinking of making a call to get rid of me.

"You think that, can help you?" I said, pointing to the phone on the desk.

I picked up the receiver and held it in front of his face with an outstretched arm.

"Were you wanting to call the police, Mark? Go ahead, be my guest, call them. Don't let me stop you, but before you do, you should probably know I've already spoken to them today. They know who you are and they know why I'm here."

Mark's face paled.

"Ready to make that call? Here, let me do it for you and then you can tell them there's a woman making a nuisance of herself on your premises who you want removed. You might want to mention it's me," I said, my index finger hovering over the number nine button on the dial pad.

"No, wait," he said.

Mark sat quietly for a moment as he weighed up his options. I could see it as clearly as a cartoon think bubble above his head with 'damage control' written in it. There were people in the neighbouring shops and offices. The murmur of their voices could be heard through the adjourning walls and this was bothering him.

Un-bloody-believable, I thought, as I watched him glance in the direction the voices were coming from and frown.

I slammed the phone back down on the desk, making Mark jump, and shouted, "Buck your ideas up! If you don't stop lying, I am going to walk out of here and go straight to the police station and make a formal complaint against you."

I intended to anyway, but Mark didn't need to know that.

Mark didn't want anyone overhearing what I was shouting about, and I was shouting like I had never in my life shouted before. I wasn't leaving until I got the answers I came for, and that, I was making sure Mark understood at the top of my lungs.

Thin walls and an angry, loud female were the right combination to make him feel the need to contain the situation before it got even more out of hand.

All out of alternative solutions, he started talking.

Diagnosed two years before he met me through partner notification, Mark had ignored the messages from the clinic at first. It was only when he had started to look noticeably ill, he finally went for a test and was immediately put on antiretroviral treatment. The contemptuous expression on his face as he spoke, indicated how he felt about having to talk about it. The resentment seeped out of him with every uttered word.

The information was given to me with a lot of short answers to my questions. Mark avoided saying anything out loud that he found too uncomfortable and this irritated me. He hadn't moved from his chair and still standing in front of him, I put my hands on my knees and bent down, putting my face as close to his as I could bear.

"I'll say the words for you, Mark, as I can see you're struggling to get your gob and your ego around them. You are HIV-positive. Because of you, I am HIV-positive. Untreated HIV leads to AIDS, which means disease and death, and that nearly happened to me."

"What do you want?" he asked, sitting stock-still in his chair, his spine as straight as a rod and hands clutching the arm rests as if the thing was about to take off. Beads of perspiration on his forehead glistened under the fluorescent lighting. It was the first time I'd ever seen Mark sweat.

"What I want is for you to give me an explanation as to why you let that happen," I answered, still standing over him.

"I don't know."

"You don't know? You're going to have to do better than that."

And there it was, the attitude. It kicked right back in, he couldn't help it.

"I am sorry, okay? I wasn't dealing with it."

"Well start dealing with it!" I bellowed as he recoiled back in his swivel chair, my voice smacking him in the face the way I had wanted my hand to.

Suddenly drained of energy, I sat on the arm of the sofa to catch my breath.

"You did tell her, didn't you?" I asked quietly, not looking at Mark. "When you heard she was in hospital. You did give her a chance, didn't you?"

"Who?" Mark asked.

"Kate," I answered, turning my head sharply towards him.

Mark's head snapped up on hearing the name. He stared back at me for a couple of seconds in silence, until he couldn't stand holding my gaze any longer.

"My God," I said. "It didn't even cross your mind, did it?"

Mark hung his head and I walked out. It was the last time I ever saw him.

25

A family lived in town who stood out for two reasons. Three, if the colour of their hair was to be included. They were Irish and all the children were girls including one set of identical twins. All five of them were redheads, ranging in lovely shades of dark auburn to strawberry blonde. I had known the girls since my early school days, the middle daughter was the same age as me.

When Katherine, Kate for short, was walking home from school with her mum and sisters, the late afternoon sun brought out the coppery hues in their hair. It was an eye-catching sight. Like a family of orange ducks, they followed each other, one flame-haired little duckling after the other.

Typical of most single-sexed group of siblings, those girls stuck together like glue but not a day went by without a skirmish of one sort or another taking place. Most of the playground fights the dinner ladies at school broke up were between two of the Irish sisters, beating the bejesus out of each other, fists flying full of each other's ginger hair.

As we all got older, parents' evening at high school was a treat if Kate's dad came along because he looked like Bono. At least he did with his sunglasses on, which he never took off even when discussing how to find the length of the hypotenuse using Pythagoras' Theorem with year ten's maths teacher. He needed to know about equations to help his Kate with her homework.

"I'll help him find out how long his length is," I even heard one of the female maths teachers say to her colleague, sitting at an adjacent table and waiting for her next set of parents to arrive.

As adults, Kate was the only one amongst her sisters who did not marry or have children. She was in the minority, as most of the women I knew in town had managed both, some more than once. I had friends who were brave enough to start again after a divorce. Second husbands and more offspring were not uncommon after a first bash at it in the twenty-something years.

Kate had had relationships, it wasn't that she was a practising virgin and saving herself for The One or her Irish Catholic Lord. It wasn't her intention to adorn a nun's habit, although it appeared she already had a habit in her life she couldn't kick.

One of the reasons that could have been attributed to her extended singledom years was she had wasted quite a few of her younger, more fertile ones on Mark. As much as they had been an on-off item for a long time, much to Kate's dismay, she could never get him to fully commit. God loved a trier and she was one.

"Be careful, Sarah," a fellow running-lover friend had said, on the night I met Mark.

"What do you mean? He's only signed my sponsor form," I'd asked back, starting a conversation about him.

"And given you his phone number. And looked at you with carnal lust in his eyes."

"So what?"

"Remember Kate from school? He strung her along for years.

She's still not over it, apparently. Rumour has it they still hook-up. At his convenience and when he hasn't got anything more interesting going on."

"Stop gossiping, we don't even know Mark," I'd said, smiling at my friend and nudging her with my elbow.

"He's rather charming and persuasive, that's all, and I would hate to see you get hurt," she'd said, looking back at Mark as we walked away to collect more sponsors.

I didn't pay a great deal of attention to the news that Kate was not very well. Probably because there was little information that went with her absence from the usual places she frequented around town. The most people knew, was that Kate had been in hospital for some time and was not accepting visitors other than her family. She would not allow anyone to see her and no one knew what Kate was ill with.

When Kate died, her parents released the news that the cause of their daughter's death was leukaemia.

The disease Kate had lost her life to, was blood cancer. There had been something wrong with Kate's immune system and her blood.

I didn't know if Kate had received a late diagnosis of HIV. Too late to save her. I didn't even know if Kate had been HIV-positive.

All I knew was, if it had been me in hospital with advanced HIV, my body being invaded and destroyed by infections and diseases, I would have played it exactly the same way Kate had at the end of her life.

26

Going to see Mark set off a chain reaction. All sorts of peculiar events happened after the confrontation I'd had with him. None of which achieved their principal goal, to make me feel sorry for him.

A local newspaper printed an article in their weekly editorial about a man who had been lifted out of a river following an attempted suicide bid. The small entry in the paper caught my eye because of the date of the incident. It was the evening of the day, I had seen Mark.

I didn't believe it was a genuine act of remorse, even before I heard Mark was standing waist deep in the floodlit dockside water, visible to passing boats and in an insulated bright red ski jacket. The jacket had been his favourite and he complained about it being ruined by the paramedic who had pulled him out of the water.

Word got around about Mark's complaining because it didn't go down too well with the emergency services and medical staff who had taken care of him afterward. One kind nurse had even gone to the bother of tumble drying his socks and underpants for him and he had still harped on about the jacket having a bust zip.

Happy to see their ungrateful patient go, Mark was discharged from hospital with his fingers and toes intact having not suffered from hypothermia, his stated intention.

Another strange story did the rounds at the same time. It originated from the young man who Mark employed. The day after my visit to the shop, Dogsbody had gone to work and let himself in, as he did every morning.

What he found inside alarmed him. A pair of step ladders lay on the floor in a position that suggested they had been knocked over. Next to them in a heap, was a length of rope. The loop tied at one end of it was a particularly chilling sight.

There was a final clue to the unfolding mystery Dogsbody had walked in on. Both items were next to the staircase in the building and directly above the rope was a broken wooden spindle, snapped in two by a force that had splintered the wood and left the remaining halves dangling at a precarious angle over the ladders.

Dogsbody looked in a triangle at what he had discovered. The ladders, the rope, and the broken spindle. He did the triangle again to make sure it looked like what he thought it did, then reported his findings to the police. He was told not to worry because his employer was alive and in hospital.

Dogsbody called the hospital and was told that after drying out and warming up, Mark would be discharged. This confused him. He didn't understand what Mark being cold and damp had to do with it. He wondered if the doctor he had spoken to had informed him of another suicide attempter by mistake.

They're at it like lemmings, Dogsbody had thought but he didn't question what he had been told by the doctor. It wasn't in his nature to challenge people in positions of authority.

Not being one to treat serious issues with inappropriate humour, I tried hard to not think bad thoughts about Mark's apparent suicide attempts. It didn't work. When I heard all these activities had taken place in the same evening, I couldn't help myself.

If Mark had really wanted to get to the sweet hereafter, he needed a hand because he wasn't very good at it. There were websites for such things, full of useful tips on suicide techniques. I could have come up with some suggestions myself had he asked. I had at one time put a lot of thought into the best way to end my own life. If it hadn't been for my children, I might have even given it a go, for real.

I was more than a little sceptical. Not being an informed expert having never tried it myself, I couldn't be sure, but I assumed a failed hanging attempt would result in some sort of neck problem. The kind that would make standing up and walking difficult.

Mark managing to get in his car and drive to the nearest port, which was a good ten miles away, having endured a cervical vertebrae injury half an hour earlier didn't seem very plausible to me. A collision with another vehicle or a lamppost would have been the very least I would have expected under these circumstances.

An obvious missed opportunity was another sign that made me suspicious. Since in his car anyway, he might as well have kept on going.

Why bother getting out? I asked myself. *He could have driven straight into the water and be done with it.*

I imagined Mark, hands gripped determinedly on the steering wheel, revving the engine then catapulting himself and the car off the dockside edge Starsky and Hutch style. Then I checked myself because that was just silly. After all the moaning that had gone on about a jacket, Mark would not have wanted any more of his possessions damaged. Driving his sports car into a river on purpose was never going to happen.

Having the forethought when in the depths of despair to put on his ski jacket, was another puzzler. He couldn't have been too worried about catching a chill if his aim was to freeze himself to death and I didn't imagine he was already wearing it. Attempting to hang himself in a ski jacket would have been a far too hot and sweaty affair, wrestling with all that rope, trussed up and padded out like Eddie the Eagle.

Mark needed someone to find the ladder and the rope, which was why they were in his shop when he had a perfectly good garage on the side of his house to hang himself in. He probably had to go to the garage in the first place to get the rope and the ladders because that's where people kept rope and ladders, in their garages.

There was probably tons of other cool stuff in there he could also have used, not to mention toxic fume inhalation.

Passing out in a car while listening to Nicholas Parsons on Radio Four was not a bad way to go. Much better than drowning when I thought about it. It didn't conjure up the same beautiful image as Ophelia floating on her Danish waters but it had other benefits. Sitting in a comfy car seat made having a little drink to relax into it possible. You couldn't do that if you were dangling from a rope by the neck, it would be too difficult to swallow.

It was a nice, private way to go. Not like trying to hang yourself in a shop from an old piece of unreliable staircase. That was just irritatingly amateurish, or a façade for a reason.

The other thing that didn't ring true about the evening was the variety in Mark's methods. I had always stayed faithful to my watery death fantasy. I couldn't think why anyone interested in self-strangulation would diversify so easily and quickly to deliberate hypothermia.

It wasn't right, they didn't go. The only thing the two had in common was that they were both showy. Mark hadn't done his research. The sad fact was when life became genuinely intolerable for a person, they usually hid away to end it. Somewhere they couldn't be found and couldn't be saved.

It was a double-up. One more for good measure. Two suicide attempts made sure someone saw something. After setting up the dramatic rope-and-ladder scene, Mark had to be an exhibitionist type of faker because he needed to be seen in the water, which was why he was under a light, wearing a bright red jacket. Someone on a ferry had seen him and called the police.

The staged suicide attempts only served to annoy me further. I wasn't fooled for a second. It was a calculated move to make me feel terrible and stop me from making a formal complaint against him. I could even imagine Mark formulating the plan in his mind while sitting in his swivel chair, *Shut her up, get her out, then make her feel guilty.*

Mark thought I was sweet and naïve. Maybe I had been once, but not anymore.

27

In the police station at the reception desk, I told the officer behind the glass I had an appointment with a detective called Linda. He looked up; we went to the same high school and he was instantly interested.

"Can I ask what it is in connection with?" he asked.

"You can ask all you want," I replied. "In the meantime, just tell her I am here, would you?"

I had changed, there was something different about me. I was angry, angry as hell, and it felt good. I wanted to know what I needed to do next and couldn't wait to get started.

Linda was nervous when we first met and shook hands. She was as unaccustomed to this type of conversation as I was. I hadn't anticipated the next person I would discuss my HIV status with would turn out to be a police officer.

As we walked along the corridor, Linda asked for my permission to introduce me to her senior officer, a detective sergeant called Joe. She explained there would only be herself and Joe involved in anything I wanted to talk about or chose to do.

Linda and Joe were plain-clothed officers and their pleasant demeanours made me wonder if they were always the detectives who dealt with cases of a sensitive nature.

They are both so ordinary, I thought, *but in a nice way.*

I wouldn't have pegged either of them as police officers. With her gentle nature, Linda particularly surprised me with her choice of vocation. Had I met her somewhere other than a police station, and she'd told me her line of work was supporting young carers or the elderly, I wouldn't have batted an eyelid. She struck me as more of a social work type than a cop.

The preliminaries had already been completed in previous meetings with Eve. As the health representative, she had been talking to senior police officers for some time about what to do with the information she knew. Already aware of the circumstances that formed my grievance, I didn't have to go into a great deal of detail with Linda and Joe about why I had asked to see them.

From the start, Joe made his feelings clear. In fact, he barely waited for my bottom to connect with a seat in the room, before doing so. In his opinion, legal action was not the answer. Given he was a law enforcement officer, Joe's attitude surprised me. I had thought my allocated officer of the law would have been champing at the bit with rage-driven enthusiasm to arrest Mark. Running out the building, arrest warrant in hand, as if the place was on fire.

Well at least he's honest, I thought. *I'll give him that.*

"It will be more complicated and distressing than you can even begin to imagine, with no guarantee of achieving anything, other than a whole load of more upset for you," Joe stated like a man who had been a policeman for a long time.

After many years of service, Joe had seen the judicial system at work and what this involved for victims of crime in court. His apprehension in putting anyone through it was plain to see, let alone someone in my situation.

"I'm sorry," Joe said, "I know that isn't what you want to hear. I just don't think a complaint of this nature would get very far. We both feel you have been through enough without your life becoming even more difficult because of a criminal investigation."

"We understand though, why you would want to make a complaint. We feel so sorry this happened to you, Sarah," Linda added gently.

"Don't," I replied.

Linda and Joe both looked at me, waiting for me to continue.

"Feel sorry for me. That's not why I'm here."

"Well at least think about it. If you decide you want to make a formal complaint, draft out what you want it to include and come back. We will do whatever you want us to, but please remember what I have said. It won't be easy," Joe said, concluding the meeting.

Linda and Joe probably didn't expect to see me again. They clearly thought to pursue any form of criminal retributive justice for a complaint like mine, would be futile. After I left the station, I went home and started to write down what I wanted to tell them on my next visit.

Back at the station a few days later, Linda wrote on the top sheet of a notepad used especially for taking witness statements as I talked, referring to the notes I'd made at home. My statement had to be recorded and handwritten by Linda, then signed by both of us to ensure authenticity. The document would then become official police evidence.

It felt strange talking to Linda about Mark and how it was between us at the beginning. Here I was, in a police station, telling a detective how lovely Mark had been to me because I wanted him arrested.

"It's important because it builds up a picture, your history with him. It fits with your complaint. This wasn't a fling or a one-night stand, you shared a relationship that should have been based on trust. Mark abused that trust over quite some time, which will strengthen your case," Linda said.

Once the background to Mark and I had been completed, more specifically, Linda wanted to record that Mark had given me the impression he had no health issues. I had never heard him say he attended medical appointments or seen him take any medication. The point being, I was completely unaware Mark was HIV-positive because he had hidden it from me.

"Did Mark ever give you any reason to worry about him?" Linda asked.

"Yes, he did," I answered honestly.

"In what way?"

"Not because I'd seen him take prescribed tablets or noticed doctors' appointments written on the calendar, nothing like that. I never had any concerns about Mark's physical health. He got headaches and said they were due to work stress, but nothing more. I worried about him in other ways."

"Can you be specific?"

"His mood. He became distant and quiet, his interest in me disappearing overnight. The contrast between how he once was with me, to being so uncomfortable around me he couldn't bear it, was a mystery to me. He physically stiffened if I touched him and it all changed so quickly, I hardly had time to draw breath let alone get used to the shift in Mark's feelings towards me."

"Did you ask him what was wrong?"

"All the time. Even though he drove me mad and his coldness towards me was hurtful, I wanted him to talk to me because I wanted to help put it right. In the end, I accepted it was over between us and told him to move out."

"And he never said anything about what was troubling him?"

"Only the usual problems at work and occasionally mentioned his parents. Did he ever mention HIV? Never. I can honestly say, hand on heart, the whole time I was with him we never even had a casual conversation about it, say over something we'd seen on the telly."

When I told Linda I felt like the stupidest person on the planet, she looked up from her notepad surprised.

"Why? You loved him, you trusted him, you gave him loads of opportunities to tell you."

"Yes, I did," I replied. "But it was too late by then. All that time, worrying about him and why he didn't want me anymore. I was already infected and strongly suspect he knew it."

Linda's face changed. "You think he knew he had infected you? When you were still in a relationship with him?" she asked.

"Yes, I do," I replied.

"What made you think that?" she asked.

"I don't suppose you've ever heard of something called seroconversion. Most people are lucky enough to not have the word in their vocabulary," I answered.

"Keep talking," Linda said, so I did.

When I had finished, Linda put her pen down on her notepad, breathed in and flopped back against the chair she was sitting on. I could see she was trying to work out how she felt about it.

That Mark, had lived with me and woken up to my face every day, and still not said a word.

28

Everyone was entitled to their own opinion.

In some HIV support and charitable organisations, wanting to prosecute a person who knowingly infected other people with the virus wasn't fashionable and this was alright with me. I didn't need any more friends and I could get by without feeling the need to be on-trend.

Linda called, two weeks after writing down my complaint.

"Just to let you know we are arresting Mark this morning. If all goes to plan, he'll be in the station being questioned by lunchtime," she said.

"Oh, okay. Thanks," I replied, not sure what else to say. If in doubt, ask a stupid question.

"How do you know he will turn up at the station?"

"Because we will be driving him there. In one of our cars after we've arrested him," Linda replied.

"Oh, I see," I said.

"Handcuffed and in the back of one," Linda added. Even though we were on the phone, I could tell she was smiling as she said it.

My mixed emotions were a surprise. I felt pleased, yet anxious at the same time about what would happen next. Also, strangely guilty, which I wasn't expecting.

Later in the day, Mark was held in a cell at the police station while the attendance of a duty solicitor was arranged. The silence that accompanied the wait must have been intolerably deafening for him. Mark asked for his interview to start without the legal advice he was entitled to.

Joe kept it brief. He only had one question.

"Are you responsible for transmitting HIV to your ex-partner, Sarah Jones?"

"Yes, it's possible," Mark said, nodding his already bowed head at his own admission.

Once provided with legal representation, Mark said nothing more. He was charged, released on bail, and allowed to go home.

Linda asked to see me and at her invitation, I arrived at the police station a couple of days after Mark had left it. It was Linda's responsibility to keep me informed of what was going on, but knowing I was in the building, Joe joined us.

"How are you feeling?" she asked.

"Nervous. What if Mark does something to get back at me? He must be furious."

"He can't, he's not allowed to. If Mark doesn't stick to his bail conditions, he'll be arrested again and that could mean waiting in prison until his court hearing," Linda said.

"He won't be looking for trouble," Joe said, joining in with the conversation. "He was very subdued when I interviewed him and didn't deny anything I read out to him from your statement."

"You read it out to him? Everything I said to Linda?" I asked.

"Yes, of course, he has to know what he is being accused of. I felt a bit sorry for the lad, actually," Joe said.

"You're kidding, right?" I said sharply.

"I couldn't help it. I just think he got caught up in a situation he didn't know how to get out of. He looked like he was going to cry while listening to some of it," Joe replied.

"Which part?" I asked.

"The part about you and him, at the beginning."

"Not the part where I nearly died, then, at the end."

"I honestly don't think he meant to hurt you and I believed him when he said, he loved you. I think he really did, before it all got messed up with the HIV stuff, anyway."

"I prefer to think he didn't mean to hurt me either, but that doesn't change anything. He did, in more ways than I am prepared to talk about right now."

I turned my head and stared out of the window in the meeting room. The view outside was in sections, dictated by the perfectly spaced metal bars that ran vertically from the top of it to the bottom. It wasn't a pretty or interesting view, but it was better than looking at Joe.

"I don't want to hear that he loved me," I said. "That just makes me feel really angry and if that is what Mark's defence is going to be, I'll have a lot to say about that."

"It's a sad situation. That's all I'm trying to say," Joe said, holding his hands up, not looking for an argument.

Linda folded her arms and threw Joe a stony look, before turning back to me.

"Well I don't feel sorry for him," she said. "Not one bit."

It didn't take long for Mark to decide what he needed to do next. Quickly and efficiently, he closed his shop and business, selling everything he could. Furniture and equipment were seen being removed from the premises at night and because of this, Mark was regarded as a flight risk by the police. Every airport in the country was notified of Mark's arrest and identity.

Trips abroad were not prohibited and his passport wasn't confiscated, but Mark did have to inform the police of any plans to travel and confirm his intention to return. If Mark made any unauthorised attempts to leave the country, airport police would be instructed to hold him until Linda arrived.

There was a word for the thought of Mark being stopped at passport control, not allowed to go on his ski trip and held in a room until Linda got there.

Satisfying.

This may have all been routine to serving police officers, but it was news to me. I looked in admiration at Linda in all her splendid ordinariness as she explained how it worked.

"I am forever having to jump on planes and chase after people who've scarpered after their arrest. They think they can avoid criminal charges being brought against them by leaving the country. Sex offenders are the worst for it." Linda rolled her eyes at the tiresomeness of it all before continuing, "They're the ones that predictably try and disappear. Spain, for some reason. That's where they're usually holed up when I find them."

"So, what happens when you get there?" I asked, wide-eyed in wonder.

"I handcuff them and bring them back," Linda replied. "It's no big deal really, just part of the job."

Appearances could be deceiving. Linda wasn't quite so ordinary after all.

29

Rumours about Mark started to pick up pace. The initial speculation around his reasons for an attempted suicide were financial problems, fuelled mostly by the highly visible closure of his business. After his arrest, local gossip turned sharply towards HIV and it didn't take long for it to reach my daughter.

Livvy.

My heart sank when I received a call from her on a night out with friends.

"Mum, this is going to sound really strange. I am out with Emily. Her mum asked her the other day, if you were okay," Livvy said.

"Why would I not be okay?" I answered.

"People are talking about Mark. Have you heard the rumours about him?" she asked.

"No, I haven't. Don't take any notice, Livvy, you know what people are like," I said.

"Mum, you might need to go for an HIV test," Livvy said, fighting back tears. "There's a rumour going around he's HIV-positive."

I was unprepared for the speed in which reports about Mark had reached Livvy, but subconsciously, I must have thought about it.

"I have already, not that long ago when I met Robin. Don't worry,

I'm fine."

I had told her the truth, I'd just missed out the part that my test had come back positive.

A small number of close friends by now knew what was going on in my life. Prompted by conversations and questions about Mark's apparent suicide attempts, it had become impossible to remain plausibly allusive about it, especially to people who knew we had remained on good terms after separating.

When they asked how they could help, all I wanted was any whispering that came my way, to be batted off in a different direction. I had thought this was a simple enough request but it was harder for them than I expected. The insistence of some people, who found this enticing piece of gossip just too tempting to leave alone, was difficult and had to be managed well.

It would have taken some front to ask me directly if I was HIV-positive. Dressing it up as false concern to friends of mine was less of a challenge. The genuinely kind people in my community said nothing, refusing to be drawn into conversations that fed on someone else's misfortune.

After picking Livvy up from her friend's house the following day, I pulled up to the house and we walked through the gate, coming to a stop on the garden path.

"It's disgusting the way people are going on," Livvy said, shaking her head in annoyance, "It's really upset me."

"What has?" I asked, knowing what she was going to say.

"Just because Mark is HIV-positive, does not mean he's going around putting other people at risk. He wouldn't do that. Mark's not particularly my cup of tea as a person, but he doesn't deserve to be talked about in that way. It's not right."

As I listened to her talking, I looked at my daughter. Her innocent, intelligent, pretty face, made me wonder if I had done the right thing. I had no way of knowing how Livvy's life would be affected by my decision to involve the police.

Listening to Livvy voice her opinion was hard enough at first. Then she really scared me.

"I am going to write to him. I am going to send him a letter offering our friendship and support. I think you should invite Mark round for dinner, Mum, he'd like that. Stuff all the rotten sods who are saying nasty things about him," my daughter said, completely unaware of the reasons why, what she was asking for was impossible.

Livvy was going to write to the man, who had been arrested for endangering my life by knowingly exposing me to his HIV, which I now had. In her letter, Livvy was going to invite Mark around to our house, because he needed friends like us.

For fuck's sake. She'll be organising a whip-round for him next, I thought, even though I wanted to sit down on the garden path and weep.

Convincing Livvy not to write to Mark wasn't too difficult. I told her it wasn't appropriate and I would text him instead, which of course, I had no intention of doing. I had stopped her from contacting Mark without having to reveal anything, but Livvy wanting to do it, upset me.

I wanted to scream at him all over again and slap his face without being stopped this time. I wanted to tell him he'd not only hurt me, he had hurt my children too.

Had Mark been standing on the garden path that day, I would have quite happily strangled him.

30

Livvy's attitude towards Mark had been commendable in the first instance. I would have felt pleased with her mature and compassionate reaction towards Mark and agreed with everything she'd said, had the rumours been unfounded.

Livvy trusted me, I was her mother and I believed in telling children the truth. I had to make sure both my children received the news of my HIV status from me. I also had to be ready to deliver it, as uncertain as I was, I would ever be. It was their faces. The thought of looking at the faces, I loved more than anything else in the whole world, when I told them.

Livvy didn't find out that day on the garden path, I put it off for as long as I could, but after Mark's arrest and as events unfolded the strain started to show. It became obvious there was something wrong and inevitably, I had to tell her.

I worried the news would disturb her so much, it would leave her emotionally traumatised and our relationship would never be the same again. I was the parent and she was my child, and that was the way I wanted it to stay. I didn't want her to view me as a victim, damaged and fragile, with an uncertain future. I should have known better because I knew how remarkable my daughter was. In fact, once I had told her, I wished I'd done it sooner.

Livvy coped with this enormous blow with the strength and composure of someone well beyond her young years. She tackled her school life and education with the robustness of a true achiever, her attendance unaffected and grades remaining impressively high as always. When she got upset, it was in private away from her peers. She spoke angrily about wanting her day in court, standing next to her mother, because this had been done to her too.

Livvy was proud of me. In her opinion, I was doing what any self-respecting woman would do and that was all I cared about. The decision to tell my daughter changed from one of my biggest fears to a new chapter in our relationship and we became closer than ever.

When I thought there was nothing more Livvy could surprise me with, feeling guilt-ridden because of everything she now had to put up with in her life, Livvy told me it had been a relief to find out.

"I'm pleased you told me, Mum."

"You don't have to say that to make me feel better, Liv."

"I'm not saying it to make you feel better, I'm saying it because I feel better. I didn't think you wanted to live with me anymore. I thought you wanted to be on your own."

"Oh, Livvy! Why on earth would you think that!"

"Because I am a teenager and teenagers get on their parents' nerves. Sometimes, I'd start an argument with you on purpose because I didn't understand why you were so quiet and we didn't talk and laugh anymore, the way we always had. It felt like I'd lost you and I didn't know why, so I thought it was me making you unhappy all the time."

"I am so sorry," I said, hugging her tight.

"Don't be sorry, Mum. I'm just pleased I know what's going on. I don't want you to feel like you should hide things from me. That's not us. I want to help," she said, hugging me tighter still.

Telling people I had been diagnosed with HIV had no definitive beginning or end, I discovered, so I went with the flow. Sometimes I thought I had finished; the people who needed to know, knew. Then other times, I felt compelled to talk about it with someone new. Telling the people who loved me was the most difficult, but it was like a weight off my shoulders once I had.

Those close to me, all said the same thing. "Why didn't you tell me?"

My answer was always the same. "Sorry, but I'm telling you now."

The question surprised me initially, then I realised, I was seeing my situation from the frame of reference of someone with HIV. They weren't and therefore, couldn't possibly understand. No one could unless they'd lived it.

Not giving people who cared about me the opportunity to go through the first year of my diagnosis with me, hurt them. The sorrow they felt, for the loneliness I had experienced, was painful for them and I got that.

Yet still, I had to ask them to accept it was for me to decide what I could and couldn't cope with and at the time, telling people had to wait until I was ready.

In the years following my diagnosis, slowly and at my own pace, I worked out how I felt about telling people I was HIV-positive.

Not everyone I knew was aware of my status, I didn't tell everyone everything about me. It was important to me that I decided who was permitted to know and I selected who to tell, it was not a given that everyone had a right to know my personal information.

HIV changed my perspective on who I wanted to spend time with. I was only prepared to invest in the people who mattered and lots of good things came out of sharing my feelings with these people.

With every person, who was the right person to tell, my life got better and my relationships grew stronger.

31

The doorbell rang; it was early evening and I didn't really want any visitors who would stop the work.

I was in the middle of redecorating and there was wet paint everywhere. Nothing cheered me up more than having a paint brush in my hand, and if this was a friend who wanted to chat, they would have to join in with the painting while they talked.

The visitor was no friend and their presence marked the point of no return. Any thoughts of withdrawing my complaint, and there had been at times out of fear or guilt, disappeared after this.

The police had managed to keep Mark's arrest out of local newspapers, some sort of deal had been made. If nothing was reported on the arrest, if or when the case went to crown court, a certain newspaper would have the story first. There was nothing that could be done about stopping the press should there be a court case. The police had a working relationship with them and a process of negotiation had already started.

When I opened the front door, the young woman on my doorstep immediately said my name enquiringly.

"Sarah Jones?"

"Yes?" I replied in the same tone.

My name confirmed, the woman proudly held up her identification badge as she introduced herself. It hadn't occurred to Sophie-something-or-other from the press, that I might have had children or elderly parents living with me when she asked if she could come in.

I wasn't sure what to do so I made something up. There had been talk of dog theft in the area. I knew this because, I had listened in on a conversation between two concerned humans belonging to a Bichon Frise and a Pug in the Post Office, a few days earlier. I hadn't realised at the time that the information would be useful for something other than making sure my dog was microchipped.

I pretended I assumed this was the reason why Sophie was knocking on doors in my street.

One of my dog's favourite things was the glorious sound of the doorbell. He would race to the door at breakneck speed and hurl himself at whoever was on the other side of it. I had put him in the kitchen and he was having his usual noisy, sweaty tantrum at being excluded from the excitement of a visitor.

"If you find out who's stealing the dogs, tell them I'll give them a tenner to take mine away," I said, but Sophie didn't laugh, she just frowned in confusion.

I could have simply told her to leave, or shut the door without saying a word, but Sophie knocking on my door made me nervous enough to be curious. I wanted to know how much she knew, how far she would go, and where her information had come from. I played along when really, I knew fine well, why there was a journalist standing on my doorstep.

Sophie was thrown for a moment at the dog theft routine, but not for long.

"The reason I'm here is not because of your dog. What I want to talk to you about is more important than that. It's delicate. It would be better if I came inside to discuss it," she said as if she was doing me a favour.

"Oh?" I replied, standing firm in the doorway.

Sophie upped her game. In a hushed tone, she mouthed the letters separately, exaggerating them for effect, "It is about, H. I. V."

If I'd had a set of cheerleader pom-poms on me, I would have shaken them right in her face while yelling at the top of my voice, "Give me an H! Give me an I! Give me V! What have I got?"

I imagined myself doing a star jump in my School of Embarrassing Diseases cheerleader uniform, shouting exuberantly, "MISERY!"

Sophie stood, waiting for my response.

"You'd better come in. I'm decorating and my paint brush will be drying out," I told her, noncommittally.

Sitting in the same place where it had all begun with Robin, Sophie started her interview.

"I wanted to give you the opportunity to comment on your complaint of HIV transmission. I gather an arrest has been made. How do you feel about that?"

With my best poker face ever, I replied, "What do you mean?"

Sophie had another stab at it.

"You did have a relationship with him, didn't you? The person in question, Mark Bennett?"

"Mark from the shop on the high street? The arty guy?" I replied.

"Yes, Mark Bennett."

"He served me once when I was in there looking for a birthday gift, but I wouldn't call that a relationship," I said, making my answer sound flippant on purpose.

Sophie looked around the room as if searching for clues and hoping something would pop up out of nowhere to help her nail a story, she desperately wanted.

I looked at the roller lying in the paint tray deliberately and exhaled impatiently.

"I need to get on. There seems to be some confusion over who knows who, and how well, for that matter. Sorry, I can't help you. Where, by the way, did you get my name and address from?" I said as I stood up to see her out.

"From work. I don't understand how I could have the wrong person. I think I'd better call the office and check my information so we can sort it out," Sophie said, wondering what to do next to avoid surrendering her position having got this far.

Good idea. You make your phone call, I'll put the kettle on, and then we'll sort the whole thing out over a nice cup of tea, I thought acidly. This silly young woman was way out of her depth and didn't even know it.

"Use the house phone," I said to her, pointing to it on a table.

"It's okay, I have my mobile in my bag," she said, scrambling around inside of it. "I'll go outside."

"I insist. It's cold out. Make your call from here," I said, standing by the table the phone was on, arms folded across my chest.

"I'd better not. It wouldn't be professional to talk about you, in front of you. If you don't mind, I'll go outside. Don't worry about coming to the door, I'll let myself out."

Sophie, the pinnacle of professional conduct, had her mobile phone in her hand before she left the room while telling me she would be back shortly.

I watched her from the window, fascinated to see if she had the audacity to come back.

While on her phone, Sophie looked at my front door to check the number. She then walked a couple of doors down to the corner of the street and looked at the street sign attached to the front of someone's garden wall. Nodding in agreement to whoever she was talking to on her phone, Sophie made her way back, walked up my garden path and rang the doorbell again.

It appeared she did.

Back on my sofa, Sophie told me she had double checked her information, she was at the right address and speaking to the right person. I didn't contradict her, I didn't say anything. She had already made her mind up she was talking to the complainant. Notepad and pencil at the ready, Sophie scanned the room again, as if looking for inspiration to get me talking.

Her eyes settled on pictures of my children in frames, leaning against a wall ready to be rehung once the paint had dried. I followed her gaze and then turned towards her.

"Do you have children, Sophie?" I asked.

Sophie was delighted, finally, we were doing some female bonding. She didn't have children yet, she eagerly told me, but would have them one day when the time was right. She looked down at the notepad on her lap, excited to get the real conversation going and start writing.

What a scoop! I could see her thinking.

I stopped smiling and stood up as I spoke.

"You do that, then one day you will understand what it's like to be a mother and the lengths you will be prepared to go to, to protect your children. Mine will be home soon, so if you don't mind, I would like you to get out of my house and not come back. I'll walk you to the door."

A blotchy reddening started to appear at the base of Sophie's neck. It rose up her throat until Sophie's face blushed bright pink. She fumbled about clumsily with her notepad and pencil, unable to get them into her handbag quick enough. After standing up, she composed herself by smoothing down the front of her skirt with two hands, before walking across the room to the door.

I had a deep-seated dislike of journalists after that. Sophie wanted to say something to hide her discomfort, the visit not being the cosy exchange she had hoped it would be.

"Sorry for being such a cunt," would have sufficed but instead, as I escorted her off the premises, Sophie commented with a sweeping gesture of her hand, "I just love what you've done with the place."

Thanks, now why don't you be a good girl and fuck off so I can carry on painting it? I thought but didn't say, as I shut the front door behind her without saying a word.

Linda was annoyed when I told her a journalist had been to my house. When she came to take a statement from me regarding the incident, she asked how I had handled it without getting flustered or upset.

"Oh, I'm getting used to it," I told her. "This is my life now."

32

I knew the journalist and the incident had to be something to do with Mark and I wasn't wrong.

An anonymous caller had contacted the paper's news desk and tipped them off about the rumours flying around about Mark. The information had made its way into a journalist's inbox and he had emailed Mark on his business email address, which was still available on the internet.

The journalist had asked Mark if he would like to comment on his arrest and to his surprise, Mark had replied. His angry response had been quite an outpour, much to the delight of the journalist. Mark had declared amongst other sanctimonious comments, that the whole business was malicious lies, started by an embittered ex-partner. He ended his message by suggesting if the journalist wanted to talk to someone, it should be me, and then had typed my name and address into the email.

The journalist had presumably sent a less experienced member of his team out to do his dirty work for him. Eager to please, off Sophie went, excited about her new assignment.

The Chief Editor of the paper denied sending Sophie to knock on my door when he was asked by Linda for an explanation. According to him, Sophie had done so under her own steam, wanting to make a name for herself by returning with a story all local journalists would want to get their teeth into once word got out about Mark's arrest.

"What do you want us to do?" Linda asked.

"I don't believe him, but if that's what he told you, I want an apology for the incident. I also want to know if he intends to discipline Sophie, for the distress her snooping around has caused me," I told Linda.

"Okay, no problem," Linda replied.

I was informed in a letter of so-called apology written by the Chief Editor, that the press had a job to do, and part of that job, was to protect the public by informing them of any dangers that may threaten their safety. He felt my regrettable situation fell into this category and for this, he was sorry. Cleverly worded to hide the stinging insult, the letter suggested people with HIV were an unwelcome entity in society. Collectively. A job lot.

The letter, which had a 'pack 'em all off to leper island' connotation to it, had not been what I'd asked for. Being a journalist, admitting being in the wrong had been too much for him. Fighting back tears of anger, I nearly tore the letter up in disgust but instead, gave it to Linda to add to the case file. If the case went to court, I wanted a judge to read it.

"And Little Miss Sophie?" I asked Linda sourly, as I handed her the letter.

"No disciplinary action but a firm slap on the wrist for the incident, or so the Chief Editor told me," she replied.

"Yeah, right. He probably gave her a pay rise. Christ, I can't stand them."

"I know, but believe it or not, press journalists are often

invaluable to the police when their investigations are done the right way. We work in partnership with them all the time. It's best not to fall out with them. That definitely would not be in our favour."

I had a new address. Mark did not need to know where I now lived unless he had a reason to find out, such as emailing the address to a journalist.

How to go about finding out where someone lived, was not something I'd had reason to think about before. I wasn't even sure if the Yellow Pages directory still existed, let alone if anyone still actually listed themselves in it. Unless someone was willing to pay for a service that would supply such information, it seemed there were limited ways to find out a person's place of residence.

The obvious one was to ask the resident. If this wasn't possible, then there was always following the resident to watch them enter their property. The only other thing I could think of, which wasn't that different, was persuading someone else to do it for you.

Postal addresses were a funny thing. I'd known friends of mine to live in the same house for years and could have done the route from mine to theirs blindfolded, but I didn't know their door number.

This was the way I explained it to Linda.

"Where does your best friend live?" I asked her.

"Park Avenue," she replied.

"What's the house number?" I asked.

"Fifty-something. I don't know actually, I've never had a reason to write it down. I take her birthday card around with her present."

"There! Exactly. Nobody bothers to memorise addresses they don't need. Mark had to have gone out of his way to find out mine. Does that not sound a bit stalkerish to you?"

Looking up an old college buddy might have been an innocent enough exercise that wasn't going to get anybody into trouble with the police. For an individual who had recently being arrested for assault, the temptation to follow and watch the complainant was one best resisted.

As part of his bail conditions, Mark had been told not contact me, come anywhere near my property, or get involved in any activities that could be viewed as intimidation. His computer and mobile phone were confiscated by the police. The items confirmed his communication with the journalist, the emails printed off, and added to the case file along with the Chief Editor's letter.

Back in the police station, Mark was asked about his email and intentions. The reason he gave for the incident didn't do him any favours.

"She needs to start thinking properly about what she is doing and stop being so naïve," Mark told the interviewing officer, furious at being picked up in a police car and brought in again for questioning.

"What do you mean?" asked the officer.

"She needs to realise just how nasty it's going to get."

"How nasty what's going to get?"

"This situation, if it continues. It'll be impossible to keep the press out of it."

"Oh, you mean the complaint against you. You think it would be better for her if she dropped it?"

"Yes, of course, it's ridiculous. All of this is and she needs to see that."

"Are you saying your email to the journalist was to assist her?"

"Yes."

"You're going to have to explain this one to me because I'm struggling."

The officer on the opposite side of the desk to Mark, leant over it as he asked, "How is revealing to the press your ex-fiancé's identity, where she lives with her children and the fact that she is HIV-positive, to her advantage?"

"To help her understand it's going to get far worse. That email was nothing more than a little taster of what's to come if she continues. I wasn't throwing her to the wolves, I was saving her from them."

The officer still didn't see where Mark was coming from, but it was one of the best lines he'd heard in a while from a Suspect Offender.

"What do you want us to do?" Linda asked, again.

"He's not getting it, is he?" I said to Linda. "Let's return the favour and help him. I want Mark arrested. Never mind me, maybe second time around, he'll start thinking about what he's doing."

"Okay, no problem," Linda said, again.

Mark refused to say how he knew my address, which was the first smart move he'd made in a while, as it saved him from sitting out his wait for a court date in prison. His contact with the journalist and emails, were a different matter.

Intimidation was viewed by the law as a personalised form of anti-social behaviour. After his second arrest in a matter of weeks, Mark was issued with an electronic tag, a curfew order, and no computer or mobile phone to play with to make his early nights go quicker.

In short, Mark was told to pack it in. Any more games, and he would be staring at four walls and a toilet bowl until a judge was ready to see him.

It wasn't in my nature to be sarcastic, but on the rare occasion when nothing else would do, I considered it an acceptable form of expression.

"Oh dear," I said to Linda when she told me how unhappy Mark had been with this arrangement. "Silly, naïve, little me."

33

HIV transmission cases were highly unusual, particularly ones that went to trial on a 'not guilty' plea. So unusual, a successful prosecution had only happened once before in the country. This became the test case that established the reckless transmission of HIV as a criminal offence. The defendant in the case did not deny transmitting the virus, his argument against criminal liability was around the issue of consent.

Consent to be touched versus consent to be put at risk due to that touch, became the debate that changed the law. The defendant had claimed he'd been open about his HIV status with his sexual partners and they had still consented to his touch. The women who testified disputed the fact, stating he had not disclosed this vital information, and they had seroconverted because of this. The jury believed the women and the defendant was eventually convicted due to his reckless behaviour towards the women.

The verdict was not well received by professionals working for HIV support organisations and would remain a controversial subject.

Due to the rarity of such cases, there was very little case law to refer to and the police force investigating my complaint had not been involved in an HIV transmission case before. In some ways, it felt like the law wasn't sure where it fit in, as there was no specific legislation.

Defendants were charged with Grievous Bodily Harm under the Offences Against the Person Act, which had been around for some time and was concerned with assault and inflicting non-fatal wounding. Two newer sections to the Act had been added since the discovery and recognition of HIV as a medical condition, establishing the reckless transmission or intentional transmission of the virus as a crime and a prosecutable offence.

Conversations regarding HIV transmission terminology with Linda and Joe became depressingly necessary because all three of us had to decide what we thought Mark had actually done. We debated the difference between 'knowingly', 'recklessly' and 'intentionally' because in the eyes of the law there was a very distinct difference.

The definition of 'knowingly' referred to Mark's full awareness of his HIV status. This would be made explicit in court by the prosecution, supported by evidence provided by the health services he accessed. The clinic appointments Mark had attended, information on HIV and advice he had received on keeping himself and any partners he had safe, the medication he had signed for and accepted, were all documented in his medical records and admissible in a court of law.

A person who behaved 'recklessly' had a gross lack of carefulness for another person's safety. Their neglect of adverse consequences made it a prosecutable offence if someone got hurt because of this type of behaviour. The term 'intentionally', just as it suggested, meant something different and way more sinister.

The maximum sentence for intentional transmission of HIV was life imprisonment. No one under English law had ever been convicted of it because it was impossible to prove. For Mark to be charged with this level of offence, I would have needed to state in an official police record, I'd heard him say he intended to infect me before performing an act of violent assault against me.

Pinning me down and declaring malicious intent while injecting me with a syringe of the virus would have done it, but otherwise, the irresponsibility of his actions whether they were calculated or not, did not constitute as intentional. The reason being, it was a consensual relationship, even though I never gave my consent to becoming HIV-positive.

Therefore, if Mark continued with a 'not guilty' plea and the case went to court, he would answer to charges of causing Grievous Bodily Harm through the reckless transmission of HIV. The only way to avoid a conviction would be to prove I could have been infected with the virus by someone else, or that he was genuinely unaware of his HIV status because of a mental state known as denial.

34

Patient confidentiality was a time-consuming business. Not that it wasn't important, as if I was ever going to be someone who disrespected a person's right to privacy, but it slowed the investigation down. People were complex beings. We made things complicated. It was in our make-up to do so.

Even though police and health authorities were pursuing the same goal, they both had a different set of rules that governed what they were, and were not, permitted to do. A bit like a footballer player and a netball player on the same team having to figure out how they can work together to get the ball in the net, without getting disqualified from the match.

Data protection policy kept HIV test results securely under wraps and the police needed this information to prove I could not have contracted the virus from anyone other than Mark. This essentially meant my ex-partners, the four contacted by Eve through partner notification, had to be contacted again but this time by the police.

Access to their medical records was needed because their HIV-negative test results were crucial to the investigation. The individuals concerned would be asked to meet with Linda and provide her with written consent, allowing the police to take a copy of the all-important test results from their medical records and add them as evidence to the case file.

Eve was not allowed to hand over any of the test results, even to the police, so a court order had to be applied for and granted before anyone could be contacted. Once this was done, it was up to Linda to make the calls and the information she presented had to be well thought out. What she said, had to be persuasive enough to get all four to participate, without giving too much away.

Linda worked on a script that stressed the importance of their consent and what their contribution meant to the case, specifically, that there wouldn't be one without it. She needed to exclude any details that would jeopardise the integrity of the case by breaching confidentiality. Aside from inadvertently saying anything that could reveal my identity, Linda also had to make sure she didn't say anything that could result in Mark taking legal action against the authorities, both health and the police. This meant more meetings and action plans to prevent anything from going wrong.

While all this was going on, a medical expert was brought in by the prosecution. She was a biologist. Under normal circumstances, the doctor's chosen professional field wouldn't have interested me in the slightest. Now, I couldn't take in the information quickly enough before firing questions at Linda, as she explained to me what the doctor's role in the investigation would be.

The biologist had recommended blood samples were taken from Mark and I and sent off for detailed analysis, a study in biology called phylogenetics. I didn't think Mark would agree to it but he did, eventually.

Linda and I were both surprised and guessed that his legal representative had talked him into it. A refusal to cooperate would have had a negative impact on whatever defence he intended to put together, but that didn't mean Mark liked having to do it.

He refused to have his blood sample taken by anyone who worked for the health authority involved in the case, claiming he believed the evidence would be tampered with. This was put down to obstinacy on Mark's part. We couldn't think of any other logical reason for it.

"What does he think is going to happen?" I said to Linda, flabbergasted at the continuing extent of Mark's self-importance. "That people who spent years studying to become doctors are going to chuck out his sample and replace it with another one of mine just to ensure a match? It's a bloody blood test, not a conspiracy plot. What a wanker."

"You went out with him," Linda said cheekily.

"Yeah, and don't I just know it," I replied.

A locum from a private medical agency was brought in to take Mark's blood sample. The young doctor didn't know why he was getting paid so well to perform a task that would take up no more than five minutes of his day. As quick as it was, he was still pleased to get it over with and leave as soon as possible, though. He'd never been asked to attend to a client in a police station before and the atmosphere had been beyond awkward.

It was all in the science. There were different strains of HIV and the relationship between Mark's HIV cells and mine was examined as closely as scientifically possible. Under the microscope, as stated in the doctor's report, the virus I shared with Mark was identical.

We had achieved all that had been hoped for. The four HIV-negative results and the phylogenetic report were in the case file. All the diligently collected evidence was enormously in favour of the prosecution.

It wasn't enough.

35

I expected an upbeat Linda and Joe at a meeting they requested at the end of the investigation. I thought a little celebration was in order after all their hard work. Cake all round, but there was no sign of cake, just glum faces.

The three of us gathered around the table in an interview room at the police station. Joe looked particularly upset, reminiscent of past occasions in the clinic with Alex and Eve.

I didn't want a softener into the conversation and asked straight away, "What's wrong?"

The case file, sent off to the Crown Prosecution Service, had been returned and rejected as court ready. The conclusion drawn by the legal experts who had examined my case was that a further investigation of another five years into my life and relationships was necessary to continue. They didn't want just post Mark relationships, they wanted the pre-Mark ones too.

If I agreed, the evidence collected would have to confirm there was not even the slightest of chances, I could have contracted the virus from someone else prior to meeting Mark.

When we broke it down, the additional requested evidence was to ensure a defence barrister could not present the argument I could've already been HIV-positive before I met Mark and my description of seroconversion was just plain old ordinary flu.

This, and sharing the same strain of the virus as Mark, would have been a big coincidence. Huge. Ladbrokes wouldn't have taken it on. Nevertheless, we weren't in a position to argue with the clever people who worked for the Crown Prosecution Service. They had decided, even though it was off the scale on the coincidence-o-meter, the gap in evidence made my case a gamble not worth taking. As it stood, anyway.

Linda was annoyed; she thought the instruction was unreasonable, delivered purposely to put major obstacles in the way of a trial going ahead.

I didn't think there was any point in getting upset about it. The legal professionals were only doing their jobs, and theirs was to decide if a case was worth the cost, time and downright hassle of a trial. The consensus had been mine wasn't.

A jury could only reach a verdict of 'guilty' if the only person possible of transmitting the virus to me was Mark and without the additional evidence, a defence barrister would have the opportunity to establish reasonable doubt in court.

Linda and Joe didn't know why the period of ten years before my diagnosis was significant, it hadn't been stated or suggested in the returned Crown Prosecution documents. We surmised there must have been a medical rationale behind it. If I had gone more than ten years without receiving antiretroviral therapy, I would have either been very sick or dead.

I could understand their frustration. Linda and Joe thought they had collected enough evidence to push it through to a trial or even a 'guilty' plea. More people meant more time and more complications.

"I don't think they get it. Did they even read the case file? Of course you didn't already have HIV before meeting Mark. The suggestion that could even be a possibility is madness. The phylogenetic results took care of that," Linda said.

"Maybe they understood the science but thought a panel of jurors wouldn't. Preconceptions about HIV still exist. It wasn't that long ago people thought you could catch it by kissing. I reckon there are still a couple of people in my office at work who wouldn't use my tea mug if they knew," I said.

"Even still," Linda said, "I've known cases to go to trial with a lot less evidence than we've collected for this one. It's because it's HIV. They're being overcautious."

"Perhaps that's a good thing. We now know the outside perimeters of what the Crown Prosecution Service expect to see as far as trial worthy evidence goes," I answered.

Linda and Joe agreed, but my positive spin on the response we had received along with the returned case file, didn't lift their spirits.

My life had been hacked, superimposed by the version Mark had chosen for me, and the two detectives sitting in front of me were upset about the way things were turning out for me.

Linda and Joe were trying to find the words to say, I would have to discuss with them a further five years' worth of sexual encounters if we were to continue, making up the requested ten-year period before my diagnosis. They looked like they had already decided this would be the end of the road for the case, that feeling deeply dissatisfied and let down by the legal system, I would refuse to entertain anymore poking around in my private life until there was nothing left private about it.

Joe looked like he would have been more comfortable setting himself on fire than asking me any more deeply personal questions.

Linda commented she wouldn't have been able to do it because she didn't have a clue how many people she'd slept with. Regardless of whether this was true or not, it was very sweet of her to say so in an attempt to make me feel better, even if it was in a tramps united front kind of way.

Their concern was endearing but I didn't necessarily see what all the fuss was about. I had thought they were going to say something way worse. I was used to receiving bad news and this news wasn't that bad. This was what my new life was like; I'd adjusted. Weird was the new normal. For me, anyway.

Aside from that, liking men enough to want to get physical with one of them from time to time, wasn't exactly front-page news. It might have been, had I stated in a police statement my sexual orientation leant towards aliens, but the reality wasn't nearly that interesting.

Enjoying talking about my sex life in a police station might have made me a bit of a pervert. It was a scenario not many people would expect to find themselves in or feel very comfortable with, unless they were happily auditioning for something that involved low-grade smut. A necessary evil to restart the investigation, I spoke and Linda wrote. Joe sat in his chair being embarrassed.

It didn't take long. A further five years' worth of relationships wasn't difficult to recount because there hadn't been that many.

"Is that it?" Linda asked, looking up from her writing.

"Sorry. I know. Poor show. I was too busy with children to have the energy or enthusiasm," I replied, smiling at them.

"Surely, that will be enough?" Linda asked Joe.

"I can't think of anything else," Joe replied.

"I can," I said.

Linda and Joe both looked at me as I spoke. "Let's double it. Keep writing Linda, twenty years should do it. I think we should push on and see where we get to, then at the very least we know we tried."

Linda finished writing, put her pen on top of the witness statement pad and slid it across the table to me. I picked up the pen and signed the bottom of it.

"Right. Now that's all sorted out and you two are feeling better, let's get the kettle on. Where's the cake tin kept in this place?" I asked a much happier couple of cops.

36

Keyboard Warrior. That's what my daughter called it. A person who played out their life and fought their battles over social media sites.

Everyone was getting into it, but I had my reservations and was not particularly a fan of Facebook. I got the concept but it didn't interest me much. I found it disconcerting that hurtful or vengeful words could be posted, visible to potentially hundreds of other people, even for just a few poisonous seconds. It could be argued that a person who did this only exposed themselves as someone of questionable moral character, but nevertheless, once something was out, it was out.

Someone with an allegiance to Mark had taken issue with me and decided to use social media to air their dissatisfaction. I was a firm believer in 'each to their own', but along with finding Mark's behaviour unacceptable, I struggled to understand how another person could find it excusable. This meant there was a conflict of interests. I wanted Mark in prison and someone else did not.

Difficulties in my already complicated life had surfaced in other ways from another source. The posts that appeared on Facebook were suggestive and vaguely threatening. Someone had something on me and it was huge. They knew my identity and HIV status.

I didn't have a Facebook account but Livvy and alarmed friends saw the posts and printed them off for me to look at. The desired result achieved, I felt frightened enough to give them to Linda, just in case the matter got out of hand. It did.

Posting comments to cause distress to another person amounted to online bullying which was bad enough but behaviour that threatened my livelihood, took the discord someone was intent on sowing to a whole new level.

I tried not to let menacing stares from slowed down vehicles spoil my day when it happened, but an incident impossible to ignore was being followed at work and shouted at, with no regard for what the surrounding people, some of them colleagues of mine, overheard.

I was aware of someone striding purposefully towards me. I sensed the anger in the steely glare and approaching footsteps but it didn't fully register until, in the large, resounding foyer of a children's hospital, a supporter of Mark's hysterically screeched their discontent in my face.

I hoped the nurse that intervened and reminded the screamer of what kind of building she was screaming in, one full of very sick children, thought I was a social worker struggling with a difficult client. I didn't want anyone at work believing the verbal attack I was on the receiving end of, was personal. HIV-positive kind of personal.

The most unlikely part of the situation was that I walked the screamer out of the nearest exit which led into the hospital car park and she let me. Not that I wanted to be in her company any longer than necessary, but I did need to get her off the premises as quickly as possible and reassure myself she had definitely gone. When I heard the sound of her car engine revving behind me, I also wanted to get back to work without being run over.

Hugging my large bundle of document folders to my chest, I quickly scuttled back through the exit I had come from. Once inside the building, I pressed my back against one of its walls as I thought about what had just taken place and what I should do about it.

It was a criminal offence to pursue a course of conduct which amounted to harassment and Joe suggested the person responsible for it should receive a warning to make sure this was understood. I was reluctant to agree to it, I didn't want any more trouble coming my way from a person so passionate about their cause they were willing to get a criminal record over it. Joe told me in his experience, intimidation only escalated if an intervention was not applied and a harassment warning was issued.

I could not understand why a third party was involving themselves. The matter was between myself and Mark. Anyone who didn't like what I was doing needed to find another way of dealing with their emotions and leave me alone. I didn't feel like this was an unreasonable request and neither did the police.

There were no further face-to-face confrontations. However, on the day Mark was convicted in crown court another Facebook post appeared which was an absolute belter. The simplicity of the wording was perfect.

"Telling lies in court is perjury," the post assertively stated. So much so, it could almost have been believed the person behind it, knew what they were talking about.

Nothing more to it, no names, no details or reference to a specific court case. The powerful sentence was a statement of fact because telling lies in court was indeed called perjury. It was also an attack on my integrity and a shame I never got the chance to thank the antagonist who posted it.

I had never considered myself a clever person. If it was their belief my ordinary, tired brain could trick a team of police detectives, a jury of twelve unbiased strangers, a high court barrister and a judge, then the person the post belonged to had paid me a larger than average compliment.

37

All it would have taken was one person not wanting to get involved and refuse an HIV test for the whole case to come tumbling down like a house of cards. Not that I had slept with fifty-two people. Out of the next batch of ex-lovers, there was a semi-professional footballer who was an ace on the field but not so great at monogamy, a Jack who had been too much of a Jack-the-lad, a few jokers, and one who turned out to be a queen on Thursday evenings at a downtown bar called The Manhole.

In summary, not a king in sight. When I thought about it all, including the original disastrous batch, I decided if I ever wanted to have a proper boyfriend again, I really needed to up my game.

The investigation had to resume and it was even more complicated this time. Asking individuals who knew they didn't have HIV for their negative test results had been relatively easy. Calling on an unsuspecting group of people to ask them to go for an HIV test, and make sure they did it, was going to be a lot harder.

Linda would be making it explicit in her conversations with them that it was not a question of suspecting they were HIV-positive, it was the opposite. The purpose of the requested tests and subsequent results were to illustrate they weren't. However, there was still a possibility someone might say, "No thanks, I don't need this in my life."

When it came to HIV, people didn't want to be associated with it. Anyone who had a partner they were serious about long-term, might have wanted to avoid any involvement with an HIV transmission case, in fear of it jeopardising their relationship. It was the potential accusations. Unjustified, but HIV frightened people enough to make even the most open of minds, closed.

"Are you telling me, you've had sex with someone with HIV, and then you slept with me?"

That kind of stuff. Judgemental comments were not hard to imagine. HIV might have been treatable, but there were no pills for the stigma attached to it.

There was another possibility that could have ground everything to a halt. We had decided to go back two decades to satisfy the Crown Prosecution Service, which was a good move and one I didn't regret but tracking people down might have proved difficult. Someone could have been living abroad or even died.

It was unlikely I wouldn't have found out one way or another if someone I had once known had died at a young age, but once we started discussing it, the possibilities kept on coming.

Because of my own without-warning diagnosis, the one that played on my mind the most was someone being coincidently HIV-positive anyway. I found myself imagining some poor, well-meaning soul, agreeing to a test only to be helpful and suddenly finding themselves plunged into the world of being HIV-positive.

I also wondered, if it wasn't out of the realms of possibility, someone revealing to Linda there was no need for a test because they already knew the result would be positive.

Strange was in. Predictability was out. That's the way it was in my new life. If either of these things happened, everything would stop. The case and the investigation would come to an end.

There were no guarantees people would willingly cooperate or that all the results would come back negative. If by chance a test result came back positive, I didn't presume the authorities would have been prepared to go down the route of the very expensive phylogenetic analysis process again, to ascertain the specific strain of the virus on any further individuals. Without even inquiring about it, I knew this was an unrealistic stretch too far.

When Linda and I discussed the variables, achieving an outcome that would satisfy the Crown Prosecution Service felt like a faraway goal. I told Linda and Eve if anyone hesitated in agreeing to a test, I would contact them myself. Linda and Eve might have been bound by codes of ethics in how much they could divulge, but I could say whatever I liked, because what I would be saying was about me.

If one of the identified individuals needed an incentive to motivate them, the human touch from me, might have been enough to persuade any disinclined members of my little faction.

As the work got underway, not only did things start to look good, it all went unbelievably smoothly.

It wasn't necessary for me to speak to anyone personally because no one had any objection in helping. Linda and Eve in collaboration found and contacted the people concerned. They were all locatable, living, willing to take a test and have their negative results used as prosecuting evidence in a court of law.

They had been gentlemanly about it when Linda explained the situation and hadn't pressed her for names or details, as tempting as it must have been.

At home, Livvy was desperate to help in some way. To demonstrate solidarity and to officially register her support for HIV testing, she insisted she wanted to have an HIV test.

"Boys have got nothing to do with it," Livvy stated impatiently, folding her arms and tapping her foot when I pointed out that she wasn't sexually active yet.

Livvy wanted to be involved, and therefore, involved she would be. I took her to the clinic to meet Eve. To humour her, Eve did a test and following the correct procedure, called Livvy to inform her the test result was negative.

"There," Livvy said proudly after her phone call from Eve, "I now know what it feels like to get HIV test results."

I could see her point, even though there was more chance of George Clooney calling me up and asking me out on a date than Livvy being HIV-positive.

Livvy's friends followed suit and she went with them, making the introductions to Eve. What with all the gossip, my exes and Livvy's campaigning, HIV testing where I lived had never had it so good.

Full to the brim with emotion and pride, I would listen to Livvy's views on the subject.

"There is no shame in going for an HIV test and if it comes back positive, it's better to know than not know," she would say.

It was as simple as that. Out of the mouths of babes.

38

As time went on, I did a lot of thinking about a lot of things. There was a lot to think about.

I would consider the guilt I had felt over Mark's arrest. It wasn't because he was my ex-partner, I felt nothing for him in that way. He had surrendered any loyalty I may have had for him, the day I found out what he had done. It was something different to this and less straightforward.

I had to reason with a part of myself that felt like I was turning on one of my own and this was very confusing. At times, I detested Mark but he was also the only person I knew in the whole world who was also HIV-positive. Even though he was the reason why I was HIV-positive.

This unsettling feeling was one I struggled to make sense of, exacerbated by the knowledge prosecution was discouraged by some organisations that existed to support people living with HIV. It felt as if somehow, I was letting the team down by pursuing a case against Mark.

The argument against prosecution was a popular ethos in HIV forums. The advice openly given on charity websites was to plead 'not guilty' to complaints of reckless transmission of the virus to avoid a custodial sentence, regardless of whether individuals believed they had committed a crime or not.

It was suggested legal action inhibited HIV testing because it acted as a deterrent. My understanding of this was, ignorant bliss was a better form of defence than a positive diagnosis where prosecution was concerned. In other words, individuals who suspected they were HIV-positive but refused to have it confirmed could carry on as normal without worrying they had committed a criminal offence if they infected another person.

If people with this selfish disposition were intent on behaving in a fashion that came naturally to them, I couldn't see how removing it from the judicial system would change their ways or help anyone who had contracted HIV because of it.

Walk in my shoes for a day, I thought, when I read the advice written by HIV professionals on their websites that Mark would have read too.

Custodial sentencing might not have been the answer, it probably wasn't, but that was a whole other different debate. Individuals who broke the law and got caught out went to prison. That was what the people who made the rules had decided. It wasn't hard. Follow the rules and don't go to prison. Mark had not followed the rules.

It was felt by some that miscarriages of justice were possible. My opinion was the opposite. Based on personal experience, I knew the lengths that had to be gone to, to get the Crown Prosecution Service to take a case file seriously. The process had been one so arduous, if cases of HIV transmission even got as far as court, I couldn't see how a miscarriage of justice would be possible. Perpetrators of this crime were rarely convicted because it was so incredibly difficult to prove, was the reality of the situation.

Another bold statement I read about was that convictions did not reduce HIV infection in the population as a whole because it promoted stigma driven by fear. Maybe it did, but this could only be measured if compared to a society which did not criminalise reckless or intentional transmission of the virus, so I couldn't see where the facts came from to back it up. Opinions based on facts. Facts based on opinions. To my mind, these were not the same thing.

I wondered if the organisations the websites belonged to had completed a survey to gather their information. A hundred HIV-positive people asked what they thought. If this was the case, it would have come as no surprise if all participants of the survey had agreed criminalisation was not the correct path to take for the better good of individuals living with HIV. I could see both sides of the coin because of my own experiences.

When Eve had warned me about the legal perils of not disclosing and infecting someone else with the virus, it made me feel like an outcast. I had enough problems without being judged as a potential offender when I hadn't done anything other than contract HIV. At the time, I'd felt people with HIV had it hard enough and legislation that isolated the group of people in society I belonged to even further, only added to the despondency.

What I found out about Mark had altered my perception. If the same hundred people were told their HIV status had been avoidable, their response to the question might have been very different. Accidents by definition were accidents due to lack of intent. Mistakes were preventable because the decisions that caused them were made consciously. I was Mark's mistake.

People who worked for these organisations may well have had their reasons for viewing prosecution as persecution but I also had mine, first hand. When the guilt kicked in, I had to keep on reminding myself that most individuals believed in doing the right and decent thing.

People who genuinely did not know or suspect they had HIV, it was unfortunate but not their fault if they passed the virus on, that's how viruses worked. People who strongly suspected or already knew they were HIV-positive and continued to put others at risk, in my opinion, were different.

The law acknowledged this as wrongdoing towards others and a criminal offence because if it didn't, there would be no responsibility and accountability to be held. Not hurting other people was the foundation civilised society was built on, the reason why it was said to young children so often. Primary school teachers all over the country, repeated daily, "You must not hit each other," for a reason.

Legal proceedings were instigated against the minority. The people who believed they were safe from complaints being made against them probably because of the understandable fear felt by their victims.

To a degree, I conceded it was inevitable I felt like this because it had happened to me. Yet still, I tried to take on board other points of view and chuck them around my brain for a while to see how they felt.

No matter how long or how often I did this for, I always came back to this.

Most people couldn't live with themselves if they thought they had hurt someone else, and then, there was the very small percentage of the population who could.

The ones who refused to admit their wrongdoing were the worst of a bad bunch. Excuses at the ready, the one that really got my hackles up was denial.

If looked up in a dictionary, the comforting text described denial as a friend. Denial was a good thing to have in certain situations because it was a natural defence mechanism. The existence of internal or external realities kept out of conscious awareness to protect a person if that was what they needed during a particularly tough time in life. Denial prevented people from becoming overwhelmed with distressing news until they were ready to accept the reality of it.

It was a genuine emotional state experienced by the parents of terminally ill children, mothers and fathers unable to cope with the unbearable pain of their child dying. I knew all about denial, I had worked with families in this much pain and supported them through it. I knew how denial worked, I had seen real tragedy.

When denial was first mentioned in connection with Mark's defence, I thought about those families and it fired me up, like a light to touch paper. Just when I had thought there was nothing more Mark could say or do that would notch up the disdain I felt for him, he'd managed it.

I wanted someone to explain to me, how Mark had come to believe he didn't have HIV when he had taken himself off for an HIV test. Presumably, it had crossed his mind when he received the phone call from the clinic that he might have it. It wasn't a wrong turn on his way to the barbers that had landed him in a sexual health clinic. Mark must have noticed he was having a needle stuck in his arm and not a hot towel wrapped around his face followed by a wet shave.

I also wanted someone to explain to me, what Mark thought he was signing for when he collected his HIV drugs from his clinic because they weren't his latest treat ordered on Amazon.

In the context of HIV transmission, I couldn't get my head around it. Perhaps it took the experience of your own diagnosis to understand how frustrating this was, how insulting to the people who lived with it, put up with it day in and day out and just got on with it, without hurting a soul.

Mark had either purposely infected me for some insanely selfish reason or was not prepared to risk disclosure, and all that he perceived would go with it, by telling me his HIV status. That was all there was to it.

I was sorry for Mark that he had been diagnosed with HIV, in the same way I felt for anyone who had contracted the virus and that, was what my guilt was all about. I empathised – how could I not? – but I had no sympathy for the situation Mark was in because it was beyond anything I could understand. He had made his decisions. It was now my turn and I was making mine.

After all the soul searching, the thought and energy that had gone into considering the issues and arguments surrounding prosecution and HIV transmission cases, none of it mattered in the end.

Mark wouldn't declare any reason for his behaviour, including denial. I never got to hear from him any explanation for the decisions he had made that had impacted so heavily on my life.

When it came to the day of his trial, Mark refused to take the stand in court and defend himself.

39

There were lots of reasons why people chose not to talk about their jobs but not many who had reasons like mine. I wasn't part of a black ops team, not like that, and it wasn't particularly in my nature to be mysterious, I just tried to be sensitive to the fact that most people did not want to think about sick children. Especially the ones who were parents themselves.

I worked for a not-for-profit organisation, a charity, that supported families who were in the worst position imaginable. Parents who had a child so poorly, their condition put their lives at risk. I asked families what I could do to help, and whatever I could, I did. Often it was simply someone to talk to.

Cancer grew in places, parts of the human body, that I had not heard of before. For example, eye cancer happened to young children, I was to find out. One of the mistakes I made early on was pre-planning conversations. More my need and concerned I would say the wrong thing, I guessed at how a parent might be feeling about their child's diagnosis and would lead the dialogue based on my assumptions. After a conversation with the mother of a three-year-old who had lost his sight to eye cancer, I never did it again.

I went to visit the family at home and when I knocked on the front door, the parent I had spoken to on the phone, opened it. The woman was pin thin and had a scarf wrapped around her head. My immediate thought was that she had cancer too, another assumption. I was later to find out she was in good health, physically anyway. As the mother of a life-threatened child, she couldn't eat because of all the worrying and her hair had dropped out because of it.

This mother had three children, all boys. Her youngest had the cancer and was at home with her. Billy, she called him. Billy had his own garden, I could see it through the open double doors from the kitchen where I was sitting with his mum. Billy was in it, having navigated his way from the house with the help of chunky ropes on wooden posts, winding a trail around the garden to different things he could play on or with. I watched him sitting in his home-made sand pit, making pot pies with his little red bucket and spade.

Billy had lost his first eye as a baby and the cancer had come back and taken his second. His prognosis was good, better than good, I knew this from his doctor. The diseased cells isolated within his eyeballs, their removal meant he was cancer free and at no more risk than any other child of it returning somewhere else in his small body.

Billy's mum wanted to talk about the garden. It had been a project that cost a lot of money the family didn't really have and was incredibly important to her. The purpose of Billy's garden was to build his confidence at feeling his way around in a safe environment so he could go to nursery school. This was a prerequisite to admission, along with the wetting himself when he felt scared, having to stop.

"They haven't got the staff to cope with his needs, as he is. It's not the school's fault. He's so young, he'll adjust. He'll forget what it was like to see things. In a few years, he won't remember that he once had sight," Billy's mum said, watching her son play through the garden doors.

"You must feel a lot of peace, knowing he is going to be okay," I said.

"What do you mean?" asked Billy's mum.

"That the cancer has gone. You don't have that worry anymore at least," I replied, still believing I was saying what a mother would want to hear.

"You mean losing Billy?"

"Well, yes."

"Billy dying was not my worst fear. Billy being blind was," she said, as she looked out at her son in his garden, feeling for the rope that would lead him back into the house and to her.

So many sad stories. The ones that made me feel the saddest, were the teenagers. Old enough to understand what was happening to them, these conversations were to become the ones I would never forget.

Suzie was sixteen and had a brain tumour. She had six weeks left to live. Her parents needed to get off the ward to go home, try and eat something, get washed and pick up some clean clothes for Suzie, before rushing back to be by her side again. They did not like her being left alone in case she died on her own, so every day, I sat with Suzie while her parents did what they needed to do, including their daughter's funeral arrangements.

The first time I met Suzie was the day after her birthday. The helium balloons with 'Happy Birthday Sweet Sixteen' printed on them, were still tied to the end of her hospital bed.

"They're driving me up the wall," Suzie said as I pulled up a chair to sit next to her.

"I bet. Parents. It's their job."

I had been about to make a wise crack about parents ruining the first half of your life, and kids, the second half. I remembered just in time that Suzie would never have children.

"Happy birthday for yesterday," I said, smiling at her.

"Thanks," she replied. "Some friends from school came in to see me with cakes."

"Was it nice to see them? Did they have lots of chat ready for you?"

"Not really. They don't know what to say. Not mature enough to know how to deal with it, I suppose," said the sixteen-year-old dying of cancer about her peers.

Sometimes I would sit with Suzie and she was too tired to talk so we'd watch some telly together. Other times she would be asleep. When she was awake and wanted to talk, we'd chat about the young celebs in the teen magazines I brought in for her. I painted her nails and we talked about clothes she had liked to wear and her favourite shops in town.

"There are so many things I will never get to do," she said one day.

"Jumping out of an aeroplane ain't all that," I said.

"I never had a boyfriend," Suzie said. My heart ached for her.

"Neither are boys. Horrible, smelly things," I said, reaching out and holding her tiny, skin-and-bone hand.

"I'll never finish school," she continued, "get a job or live on my own because I'll never grow up."

Suzie the eternal child, died before the balloons announcing her sixteenth birthday were taken down. A nurse was cutting them off the end of the empty hospital bed the last time I walked into her room.

"I didn't get to say goodbye," I said to her dad.

"She did," Suzie's dad said as he gathered up the rest of her things "She asked me to give you this, please take it, she's left one for everyone who stayed with her to the end."

Suzie had been a musician before she became ill. I watched the recording her dad had burnt onto the CD when I got home. She was singing a song that she had written and playing her guitar. Suzie had been beautiful before her illness. Beautiful and talented, the way she wanted to be remembered.

I had indeed, seen real tragedy. I had bared witness to other people's grief in its rawest form. Grief in response to the death of an innocent child, their own child.

Some lives were shortened by an undeterminable factor that was governed by a power difficult to understand and accept. If there was such a thing as fate, then at times, it was a cruel master.

Controlling the fate of others was a dangerous game to play. Nevertheless, some people still bestowed themselves with this power. It was a potent mix, power and control.

Loss of life came with a price for the loved ones left behind. Whether that be a mother, father, sibling or child, it had a toll. It changed everything, forever.

The lives of the people in my family had nearly been changed forever and I was convinced, denial, had fuck all to do with it.

40

The results from the extended police investigation were impressive and because of this, my case started to attract the attention of high-ranking police officers. It could no longer be dismissed as one doomed to fail and this made it interesting.

Permission was granted for Linda to undertake other lines of enquiry, in the first instance to strengthen the case. Even though Linda believed the evidence supporting my complaint was now indisputable, she was willing to take on further investigation to avoid the disappointment of the case file being returned yet again, having failed the scrutiny of the Crown Prosecution Service for the second time.

Linda had been instructed to search for any further victims of the same crime. She was going to look for other potential complainants who were unaware they had been exposed to HIV infection. This decision, in part, had been made because of increasing concern regarding Mark's defiant refusal to submit the names of any of his past partners to the authorities. He didn't deny having sexual relationships, or that he had put other women at risk for that matter. He just brashly stated when asked, that it was nobody's business but his.

If his attitude was a demonstration of his displeasure at the way he perceived he was being treated by the authorities, his protest didn't assist him, because all his stubbornness did was increase suspicion and instigate a more thorough investigation into his private life.

The police began examining the possibility that Mark was hiding a string of prosecutable offences. If there were other women who came forward and tested positive, Mark could have been looking at consecutive prison sentences for each individual offence, putting him in prison for years.

Linda had to start somewhere, so she started with her most available source of information, which was me. I knew of three women Mark had been involved with in the years following on from us separating and aware of these relationships for an assortment of different reasons.

The first one he had told me about himself. We had run into each other on a night out, not long after breaking up, and had done the usual polite pleasantries. Mark was with his new girlfriend and introduced me to her. I remembered her first name and vaguely what she looked like. It wasn't much to go on, but Linda was grateful enough when I told her all I could recall.

The second was easy because I knew her, as did the police. Nevertheless, I described for the purposes of the statement Linda was writing, how I had already given her name to Eve along with Mark's immediately following my own diagnosis. They were a couple at the time and it had felt right to tell Eve about her, just in case. If Mark ignored Eve's calls, a woman wouldn't, was my reasoning.

I had no clear picture of the third woman or any details that would make her immediately identifiable, but I knew she existed and had been in Mark's life more recently. Facebook and gossip had provided people locally with this information, mostly generated by Mark's previous partner.

Hell hath no fury like a woman scorned, and all that. No one was angrier than a woman rejected in love. Unable to reign in her jealousy and furious at being replaced, Mark's ex-girlfriend had been very vocal about it around town. All I knew I told Linda. I didn't have a name but I knew the most recent object of Mark's desire was a lot younger than him, slim and pretty, and of Asian descent.

When Linda contacted the women, all three confirmed they had been unaware of Mark's HIV status while in a relationship with him. The two that wished to make a complaint against Mark tested negative. Both women wanted to meet me which I politely declined. They had been lucky but were limited to what they could do about the anger they felt towards Mark because being put at risk was not a prosecutable offence in England. Had their relationships with him taken place over the Scottish border, they both could have pursued a charge of reckless endangerment against him for exposing them to the virus he carried.

At Linda's suggestion, they both submitted statements detailing just how lucky they had been after their encounters with Mark. Their statements were added to the case file to be re-submitted to the Crown Prosecution Service as supporting evidence. The message being, Mark's cavalier attitude towards the women he chose to have relationships with was dangerous, and it had to be stopped before anyone else got hurt.

The first woman remained angry for some time to come. The opportunity came for her to vent her rage after Mark was convicted. She approached a national tabloid newspaper and her interview was printed along with pictures of herself and Mark as a couple. She got her chance to call him all the names she wanted to and they weren't very nice.

Mark's more recent girlfriend had a different way of dealing with how she felt about him. After Linda had taken her statement, she immediately moved out of the area. Not wanting to be anywhere near Mark or anything that reminded her of him, she moved back home to a different city somewhere else in the country. The move put a good two hundred miles between herself and the man who there by the grace of God, had not managed to infect her with HIV.

The other woman had made her choices and I just did my level best to stay out of her way.

There it was, no more witnesses for the prosecution. Even though we all now knew, I hadn't been exclusive in Mark's risk-taking.

Mark had decided to live his life free from the shackles of responsibility HIV brought, which meant he didn't have to tell anyone or change anything. I wondered if Mark had considered himself untouchable after all the years following on from me because nothing had happened. Nothing at all. No accusations, no whispers, no questions asked. There had been no mention of HIV that I knew of, at any time in my town. Even when Kate died.

If Mark had once felt safe in the knowledge fear shut people up, he didn't anymore. I liked talking and I was good at it, especially when angry. I really hoped he rued the day, he'd met me. I wanted him to shudder at the thought of me, jump at the mention of my name, but most of all, I wanted Mark to be held in trepidation of what I was going to say next. To a judge and jury, if necessary.

Silence had protected him for too long. Sex had been his weapon. Words were mine.

What seemed like a lifetime later, the Crown Prosecution Service was finally satisfied with the information and evidence that had been presented to them. Mark was answerable to all I had stated in my complaint against him. If he formally entered a plea of 'not guilty', the case would be tried in crown court.

41

Someone had been busy. A person who had taken up a role as part of Mark's defence team as an unofficial, unpaid Private Investigator.

Linda called me to arrange a time to see and speak to each other, which wasn't unusual. Our meetings had grown increasingly frequent as time grew closer to a trial date. We had stopped meeting at the police station because Linda was concerned it would be noted by other people in the building who might link me to the investigation.

Instead, we met at my house which wasn't a problem. There was nothing about Linda, neither the clothes she wore nor the car she drove, that would have screamed out 'police officer at her door' to the neighbours.

Information was now being exchanged between the prosecution and defence representatives. When Linda arrived at my house, the main reason for her visit was to discuss how I felt about a request to release my medical records to the defence.

I didn't have to, but to demonstrate my willingness to cooperate Linda suggested I did, and I agreed with her. I wanted to give the impression I was open and communicative. My transparency would be noted and was important; I had nothing to hide. I assumed this was the usual protocol in cases that involved a lot of medical information and all the defence wanted was confirmation everything about HIV recorded in my medical records, matched up with what I had told the police.

I understood why Mark's legal representative would want to cross-reference dates and details with the police statements I had put my signature to, as validation what was recorded was the truth. He was professionally obligated to do so. It was his job to spot any discrepancies and this was fine by me because there weren't any.

I trusted the legal system. It didn't enter my thoughts that a defence barrister would be allowed to use information from my records that had nothing to do with the case, for the sole purpose of destroying me in front of the jury. If it had, if I'd been aware of what he was going to do with it in court, I would've told the defence what he could do with his request for my personal information.

Linda handed me a pen and I signed the consent form that delivered my medical records straight into the hands of the defence because I couldn't think of a reason why not to.

The other reason for Linda's visit was to discuss with me a list of names that had been submitted as evidence for the defence. Someone on behalf of Mark had gone to a lot of bother finding out certain things about me, my private life being the focus of the questions asked. Shared acquaintances were common where I lived and there were unlimited opportunities for people to meet and talk.

The document Linda had brought with her contained a copy of a list. On it, were the names of people I knew one way or another, that the Private Investigator had provided the defence with as a result of her loosely-based research.

The list was in her opinion, all the people I could possibly have had sex with.

I had managed some degree of success with the opposite sex in my lifetime but the list was way out of my league. It suggested I threw myself at men like there was going to be no tomorrow and I intended to exit the world with a bang. Or possibly a gang bang because there were a lot of people on it, to get through one at a time.

I could totally see where the Private Investigator was coming from with the list. The aim and objectives of it were obvious, too obvious to be the clever move she thought it would be. The aim was to discredit me and the list provided several objectives to achieve this goal. The objectives took the form of the men on the inventory. They were listed in no particular order, which I thought was sloppy, given the time it must have taken to compile the information.

A tool intended to stoke up trouble and doubt, the list suggested there were others who should have been included in the investigation that hadn't been. It implied I was hiding an energetic sexual past with no way of knowing for certain who I had got the virus from because there had been so many enthusiastic participants.

Disreputable and untrustworthy. An unreliable witness. That was me, according to the list, the Private Investigators personal contribution towards Mark's defence. More than likely put together in the hope my complaint would be withdrawn.

Skulking around in someone else's life was creepy. In her eagerness to assist Mark, this seemed to have escaped the Private Investigator. I was the only witness in a case the police had put a lot of time, effort, and therefore public money into. I was not a suspect and therefore not under investigation. It was not me who had committed a crime.

Linda was not allowed to show me the actual text because it was a copy of an official document for the defence.

"I know some of the people on the list. The Garys are on it. There are others I haven't heard of before, can you tell me about your involvement with them?" she asked.

"Let's have it then," I said, holding out my hand.

"I can't show it to you," Linda replied, flicking the document up against her chest as if I was trying to copy her homework.

"How do I talk about the people you want to know about, if I don't know who you are talking about?" I asked.

Linda frowned. "I see what you mean. We're going to have to get around this somehow. Have you definitely told me about all of your sexual relationships?"

"Come on, Linda, how can you ask me that?"

"Because I have to. Have you?"

"Yes."

"Right. Well in that case, I am going to have to read out the following names. Who is Gregory Lamb?"

"Lambchops."

"Sorry?"

"That's what we called Greg at school. Lambchops. I helped him with his paper round in middle school."

"The extend of your contact with this person was his paper round when you were ten years old?"

"That and youth club on Thursdays in high school."

"But you never had sex with him?"

"With Lambchops? No of course not."

Ex-boyfriends, people I had once dated, men who had attended the same schools as me, friends of mine who happened to be male and the odd husband who belonged to a friend thrown in for good measure, were the names that made up the list. Along with Robin, there was even a friend of his in the mix who worked in a computer shop. I'd never been intimate with him but he had once given my laptop a right good seeing to.

Some of the connections were so tenuous, I had to work out if I'd ever met them, let alone had sex with them.

"The Texan," said Linda.

"The Texan?" I said back.

"Yes, The Texan. There's no name, that's all that's written on the list," Linda replied, looking down at the list again to double check this was the case.

"Anyone from Texas or one specific person?"

"One specific person. Not a Texan, The Texan. I don't think you're taking this seriously."

"I am taking it seriously. I've never been to Texas."

"You don't have to go to Texas to meet a Texan."

"Are you sure? Have you ever met a Texan around here?"

"Well, no. Who is it then? Do you know?"

I thought about the question for a moment, pinching the end of my chin between the knuckle of my forefinger and thumb as I concentrated.

"Is there anyone called Nigel on the list?"

Linda looked down at the document now on her lap and I watched as she ran her index finger down the long list of names.

"Nope. No Nigels. Why?"

"I had a lunch date with someone from The Midlands once. He wore a pair of cowboy boots, the reason why I didn't see him again. That's all I've got."

The Private Investigator must have got muddled up and this was who she meant. Randy the horse rancher from Dallas was really Nigel the pipefitter from Scunthorpe. Linda read out the rest of the names. She didn't bother recording anymore of my responses after The Texan so it didn't take much longer.

"Who the fuck does she think she is? Nancy Drew? How dare she?" I said, when Linda had read out the last name.

"You don't think this was Mark?" Linda asked.

"No. Mark wouldn't know any of that stuff. I know who wrote the list, don't you?"

"Yes, I just wanted to hear it from you first. What do you want to do about it?"

"Like what? She has already been told to leave me alone. You know what, Linda? I almost feel sorry for her. Mark is using her and she doesn't even see it. How stupid can some people be?"

"Well, I could put a case forward to have the list withdrawn as evidence given what we have discussed. It would be up to the defence, but I kind of think it works in our favour. It's smacks of desperate. I think we should play them at their own game and leave it right where it is."

And that was what we did. Nothing. The list stayed put as evidence for the defence and when it was read out in court, by the prosecuting barrister, she used it to the best of her advantage. I gave my explanations of how I knew the people on it and didn't mind when at times, the judge had to stop the jurors from laughing. The list helped them get to know me and they liked me all the more for it.

The other disgraceful actions of the author of the list were used by the prosecution too. It was poetic justice. All of it, all together, looked terrible. For the defence. The Private Investigator's misguided acts of loyalty had not helped Mark one bit.

It seemed by the look of incredulity on the faces of the jurors, they had made their own minds up about Mark and his associate before we had barely got started and the irony of it was, all the work had been done for me.

42

I wondered why some people did it to themselves.

Why some people became internet trolls, stalkers and screamers, or pretended to be Private Investigators.

When it came to relationships, I couldn't understand why some people chose to become emotional litter bins when all they were going to take home was someone else's trash.

I surmised, it could only be because it was a direct reflection of how they felt about themselves and that was sad.

I felt annoyed with myself because I was letting it get to me. I worried about who I might run into in public places, where there was the potential for another distressing scene involving a lot of shouting about HIV.

My own behaviour had started to change in an unhealthy way. When out, whether in shops, restaurants or the gym, I carried out my own mini surveillance operation on entering a building to see who was in it. I would look around me furtively, to check I wasn't going to be ambushed by the enemy. I dreaded being on a rowing machine at the gym and a certain someone plonking themselves on the one next to it. I felt a sense of relief on completing a supermarket shop without bumping into someone I didn't want to at the deli counter.

It would have been difficult to know for sure, but as far as I was aware, my identity and HIV status had not been openly revealed. I knew I was being talked about, but at least the offensive remarks being made about me were contained to a degree. I assumed the warnings from the police had curbed any brazen public announcements. I wasn't under any illusion it was because of an awakening of self-awareness or a guilty conscience. Way more likely, the prospect of being put in front of a judge on a charge of harassment.

The surreptitious hints that went with the insults, were more troubling than the insults themselves. I didn't want anything to do with someone who chose to spend their time standing in Mark's corner, but it wouldn't have taken much for local people to work out why a campaigner of his was far too interested in me. Whatever Mark was doing, or promising, it was working because he had a devoted supporter onboard who could just not leave it alone.

I couldn't respond to the things being said about me without compromising my privacy and possibly the investigation. I got the impression, if I retaliated and spoke out, all it would achieve was a returned torrent of abuse on social media and I needed to avoid that. I could not expect someone who was worryingly out of control to control themselves, any more than thinking efforts to reason with the unreasonable ever worked.

I wasn't interested in the reasons for the unwanted attention I was receiving. I didn't care why other people chose to make the emotional ties they did. I didn't want to think about it, I had enough to think about, but it was hard not to. The preoccupation someone had in entangling themselves in the drama had become part of a storyline so strange, I started to wonder what it would look like, if I ever got around to writing it all down one day.

A lover of limelight was welcome to it, I certainly didn't want it. If attention was what they craved, they could have it. The frustrating part was the nudging in on a narrative that did not belong to anyone other than me.

The cheap shots were that alright, so cheap they were given away to anyone prepared to listen. Throwing unsubstantiated insults around about me was easy, especially because I was unable to defend myself. Using the written word to describe and convey a story of major significance to the individual telling it, was a whole lot harder.

My parents had always told me if someone was being unkind, to hold my head up high and remain quiet because a silent dignity said more about a person than the ill-intended words spoken by another. Throughout the duration of the investigation, the trial and for years afterwards, this was what I did. I knew my worth and the people who mattered knew it too.

I was quietly confident, one day, I would find the strength and get the opportunity to express myself in a way that was right for me.

43

As expected, Mark declined to change his plea to 'guilty' and a preliminary date was set for the trial to begin in six weeks, leaving a short window of opportunity for Mark to reconsider his position.

"Defendants often change their plea as late as it can possibly be left, apart from the ones who expect to be convicted and plead 'guilty' straight away to avoid a longer sentence. Where there is less chance of a conviction, defendants hang out in the hope of submission by the victim," Linda explained.

"Defendants are willing to chance it and risk getting a maximum sentence?" I asked.

"Quite often, yes. It's a game of bluff to see who can withstand the pressure for the longest. Once it gets this close to a trial date, defendants tend to stick with it because they have lost the chance of a reduced sentence through an early 'guilty' plea. The only move left is to wait and see if the victim buckles first by not attending court."

"Why would a witness get so far with their complaint, to not go through with it on the day of the trial? I don't understand."

"Good. I'm glad you don't understand because it happens all the time. I've often arrived at a witness's house to take them to court on the first day of a big trial, only to be turned away. It's not uncommon for people to withdraw their complaint on the morning of the trial, especially victims of crimes of a sexual nature."

I thought about what Linda had said because my crime scene, albeit consensual, had been one created by the business of sex. I wondered if I fell into the bracket of people who more often than not, closed their front door on the officer collecting them for court and their opportunity for justice. I asked myself if I should feel terrified at the prospect of appearing in court as a witness, the reason being, I didn't. Any agitation I felt was because of the lack of a definite plan so I could organise myself.

"How am I supposed to predict if a trial is going ahead or not?" I asked Linda.

"You can't. Mark may not know what he is going to do yet. At the moment, he's doing what most defendants do in this situation, sitting it out to see what you do. I think we should start planning on there being a trial, and if Mark changes his plea at some point in the next six weeks, it's a bonus," Linda said.

With this advice in mind, I had a short pre-trial 'to do' list that needed my attention.

Item number one on it was my work dilemma. I would need time off to be authorised and flexible. None of my colleagues knew I was taking Mark to court or the reason why.

I could have disclosed nothing and requested annual leave but this was risky. It could have been refused because someone had beaten me to it and already booked the same days off I needed. It was possible the trial could last more than a week or change to another date and I couldn't keep booking days off because I would run out of them.

I didn't know what to do, short of pulling a sickie, so I decided to be done with it and tell my manager everything. There was no cutting corners or slicing bits off out of embarrassment, I couldn't tell her half the story. One morning at work, I made us a cup of tea, sat down in front of her and blurted the whole lot out.

My manager's reaction was a surprise. Her calm, reassuring manner was exactly what I needed. If I had shocked her with my news, she hid it well.

"I am so sorry this has happened to you. What can I do to help?" she asked.

We deliberated what to tell everyone else at work. Jury service was suggested but quickly dismissed as too close to the truth. The matter was settled with two weeks' holiday leave authorised by her, starting on the first day of the trial. If I needed any more time off work, she would think of something to tell the HR department that didn't involve mentioning anything about a court case or HIV.

I had always liked going to work. Even though everyone grumbled about Monday mornings, I suspected most people secretly appreciated them and moaning about them was an integral part of it. It was the routine and opportunity to talk to people without the social pressures of entertaining or being the entertained. Everyone was there for the same reason and even though the camaraderie was enforced, lots of genuine friendships came out of having a job to go to.

Even the Monday morning following my diagnosis, I still went to work. Not the usual start to my week because first I had to meet my HIV doctor in a sexual health clinic. But still, after meeting Alex, off I went because that was what people did on Monday mornings.

The closer it got to a trial, the more I found being in the presence of other people difficult. I stepped right back from the usual friendly banter that went on in the office and spent as much time as I could on my own. Given a choice, I would have stayed at home and not talked to anyone at all, but this was a luxury I couldn't afford. Sitting around the house like a recluse may have been my favourite pastime but it didn't pay the bills.

I was aware that once again, I was isolating myself, but for different reasons this time around. Leaving the house had become increasingly problematic as the investigation progressed and even though I craved the comfort of company, I didn't want to be around other people at the same time because it was too stressful.

I might have been fun to be around at one time in my life but I wasn't anymore. Inadequate and awkward in social contexts, I had a party phobia and dreaded an invitation I couldn't get out of. I was dull and I knew it. Pretending to enjoy myself during social gatherings was not the answer because the acting was so toe-curlingly painful, it made time go even slower.

My somewhat quirky but quick wit disappeared into a self-conscious hole when I was in company. It landed with a thump at the bottom of the pit and lay there, amongst the dusty remains of other quick wits that had died from the same thing. A severe case of being boring. I didn't know what to talk about because I didn't have a reservoir of regular chatty stuff to fall back on, so when I had to go out, I was quiet. People didn't know quite what to say to me. I noticed the only question I got asked was, "How's the kids?"

I had become one of those women who had nothing to talk about other than their offspring and I knew why that was. Guarded and stiff, I was always on high alert that a conversation might spin dangerously in a direction I didn't want it to and would find difficult to get out of.

Permanently pre-occupied with thoughts of a trial, I was worried I came off as a bit odd in social situations so most of the time it was easier to just avoid them, but this was a double-edged sword. Look odd or feel lonely. Sometimes I took the lesser of two evils and when avoidance got too lonely, was tempted enough to go out with friends to busy places, the sort of places I used to go to when I liked my life. Night-time places, where people had had a drink or two.

This type of environment was perfect for disaster to strike from a well-intended but unexpected source. People were curious, that was obvious, they looked in my direction for just a little bit too long. I would tell myself no one knew for sure what was going on, but then occasionally, someone would hedge their bets with a random comment.

"Respect."

"Sorry?"

"For what you are doing about the Mark Bennett situation. Respect."

Comments like this, that left me nowhere to hide, were the hardest. I resisted being pulled into conversations I didn't want to have with people I didn't know that well, by denying any knowledge of what they were talking about.

These short exchanges would end the evening. For me, anyway. Perplexed as to how people could think I would be prepared to discuss something so important with them, I would suddenly feel very tired, get in a taxi and leave. The feeling of relief, as I put the key in the front door, was like a drug being released into my veins. I was home and back to the solace of being on my own again.

For these reasons amongst many others, counting down the weeks to the trial kept me going. I started to look forward to it and could barely think about anything else. My life was hung in suspended animation and I fantasised about a future that blossomed with good things when it was all behind me.

The trial became my focal point to another new beginning and I promised myself every day, once it was all over, I would start living again. I would allow myself to find some happiness in whatever form that took because I had worked for it and deserved it.

44

I'd always been a lover of lists. I used them as working documents to keep me feeling safe. When everything on one was completed I felt such a sense of satisfaction, sometimes I wrote it out again just for the pleasure of the ticking. Lists rocked. They helped me convince myself I wasn't an overachiever at fucking up.

Now that the first item was ticked off my pre-trial one and I had my authorised leave from work arranged, it was Linda's turn to action number two.

Item two on the list was a visit to the crown court building in the city. Having a look-see was something the police often did with witnesses, in what were considered to be big cases. We went on a quiet mid-week day in Linda's car, so she could show me where she would be parking up on the day of the trial, her chosen spot getting us in and out of the building as discreetly as possible.

The purpose of the visit was to allow me to see what the inside of a courtroom looked like, based on the premise it would make appearing in court as a key witness less daunting when it came to the real event. A measure to avoid police officers such as Linda leaving alone when she arrived to collect witnesses on their big day, it limited the chances of a disappointing no show.

I had never been in a court building before and was pleased to see the rooms were smaller than I had imagined when we looked inside an empty one. Linda asked if I would like to watch ten minutes of an actual trial taking place. I was curious, but not quite sure what she meant. Linda quietly opened the door to another courtroom and I followed her inside. I was taken aback at just how open, an open court was, astounded we could walk right in on a real court hearing.

I sat down on a bench in the public gallery, next to a woman who had her coat pulled tightly around herself, as if for protection. In her hand she held a crumpled tissue, it was pressed tightly up against her mouth and the underneath of her nose.

The woman was watching the person in the witness stand, a younger woman who could have been her daughter. I wanted to ask her if she was alright, but I couldn't because no one was meant to talk during a preceding other than the participants. The sign pinned to the wall above us with 'silence' written on it in large letters, made that clear to anyone who might have been tempted.

The witness's complaint was she had been assaulted by her ex-partner. He was also in the courtroom, behind the glass wall that separated him from the rest of the people in the room. Visible from the public gallery, I could see him, sat with his arms folded across his large chest as he stared at the witness. Standing stiffly in the witness box, the woman purposely did not look back at him as she tried to answer the questions being fired at her without getting upset.

I felt terrible for the witness, unlike the defence barrister. Trying to get her to admit, the domestic violence she had suffered resulting in her ex-partner's arrest was her fault, he spoke to the woman in the witness stand as if she was something on the bottom of his shoe.

"I put it to you, you hit your ex-partner first. He pushed you to defend himself as you continued to strike him. That's what really happened, isn't it?" he barked at her forcefully, not giving her time to respond before starting again.

"Your complaint to the police was not because you were fearful of your partner's actions. Spite was the driving force behind it. You might not like it, but fathers have rights," he stated loudly, mainly for the jury, before accusing the witness of using anything she could to refuse his client access to their children.

When we left the courtroom, I was upset by what I had seen and heard. I found it hard to believe barristers could speak to witnesses so aggressively without being reprimanded by the judge.

"He was horrible. Why did the judge not stop him from going on at her like that?" I asked Linda.

"That was unlucky. It wasn't my intention for you to see something like that. I'm sorry," she replied.

"Why? What do you mean?" I asked, unsure why Linda was apologising.

"What you saw and heard, unfortunately, was a fairly regular cross-examination style."

"What? Making up a storyline to belittle a witness? How the hell is that legal?"

"Begs belief, I know, but sadly it's the way it works in a courtroom."

I tried not to think about the visit after we left. I couldn't afford to get scared. Not now, it was too close to me being the person in the stand.

45

I had some homework to do, to complete the next task on the list. I needed to write a Victim Impact Statement, which the presiding judge would read in advance of the trial. It was my opportunity to ask for any special conditions to be considered and state my reasons why. After the visit to the court building and discovering an open courtroom was precisely that, my thoughts were dominated by how I was going to manage my life after a very public trial.

Linda was unconfident how much difference stating my concerns in the Victim Impact Statement would make. She had already enquired about a closed court, the term used when no access was given to the public and the courtroom door locked once a trial had begun. Her request had not been well received by the judge. Closed courts were rare and usually reserved for very specific reasons concerning the need for high security. An act of terrorism case was the example Linda used when I had asked what that meant.

Giving my evidence via video link was an alternative to being in the courtroom, the presence of a monitor screen instead of me in person, but this wasn't without disadvantages. Something was lost when a witness gave their evidence remotely, the emotion and human element diluted.

There was no getting away from it, my physical presence during the preceding would undoubtedly be to the benefit of the prosecution. Linda had already negotiated the witness stand being screened off while I was in it, which the judge had agreed to. She believed this was the full extent of his generosity, as far as special considerations were concerned.

My voice would be heard but at least I would be out of view of everyone other than the judge, jury and two barristers. Mark and the audience in the public gallery would not be able to see me while I gave evidence.

I sat at my kitchen table, pen in hand, looking at the blank document Linda had given me with the title 'Victim Impact Statement' at the top of it. I had to describe how finding out I was HIV-positive had impacted on my life and was wondering where to start.

Oh, just get on with it, I thought to myself after a while. *Tell the man how you feel. Write the bloody thing rather than sitting here worrying about sounding like an idiot.*

And I did, I told him. I told the judge what it was like being me. I poured my heart out in words, crying as I wrote them, a couple of big, wet splodges hitting the paper as if sealing the emotion that I found surprisingly easy to portray once I got going.

I finished with a paragraph about how important it was to me that my parents were spared from the news of what had happened to me, because if they found out, they would spend the rest of their lives worrying about me. I told the judge this was what mattered to me most, along with my children's lives being as unaffected as possible by my chosen course of action.

The case had received a huge amount of public interest. It was unavoidable local people would turn up at court on the day I was giving evidence. I would be instantly identifiable as soon as I started speaking. I asked the judge, and I knew this was a big ask, to not allow members of the press to be at the trial and grant me a closed court.

Linda would later describe to me a visible shift in attitude, a softening in his eyes when the judge read my Victim Impact Statement. She had been standing in front of him, waiting for his response, and could see his expression changing as his eyes moved along my sentences. Writing about my feelings had made me a real person, someone's daughter and a mother instead of a case number, and it was enough to make him change his mind.

A member of the press would be present to report the findings of the case, that was how it worked. However, there would only be one chosen by the judge, with strict instruction from him what reporting would be permitted.

Provision would be made to ensure I was completely out of view from the public and any press photography on my arrival and departure from court.

I would be known only as 'X' in the courtroom, with no identifiable features in any of the inevitable editorials in newspapers.

The room would be secured with no access to the public gallery, protecting my identity and eliminating the risk of any upsetting outbursts of unreasonable behaviour from anyone favouring Mark during the hearing.

On the morning of the trial, the judge himself would put a notice on the door and a security guard in front of it, as he told Linda.

I couldn't quite believe it, I had been granted a closed court. I hadn't been expecting anything let alone this and felt so incredibly grateful to the judge I could have kissed him.

A big sloppy wet one, right on the chops and long enough to make his specs steam up.

46

With only a week to go, Mark's plea remained 'not guilty' and therefore one more thing had to be done before the trial. The very last item on the 'to do' list was to meet the Chief Crown Prosecutor.

I was expecting an older, stern-looking person when I met Carolyn and was surprised to find her quite the opposite. She had requested the meeting to introduce herself and answer any questions Linda and I had before the trial.

A woman had purposely been selected for her gender and Carolyn had wanted the case. She had a passion for seeking justice, particularly when it involved vulnerable female victims. Linda had more detailed questions than me, all I wanted to know was what I would be asked in court. Carolyn side-stepped my question, simply stating to be myself in the witness stand and not to worry about showing emotion.

"Cry, get angry even. Emotion is always good in front of a jury," she told me.

This response confused me because it wasn't what I had asked her.

Why would I cry or get angry? I thought.

I wasn't on trial. I was curious about the questions I would be asked because I couldn't see what was left to talk about. It had all been covered in the recorded evidence, which I assumed would make my appearance in Mark's trial a very short one. In and out. That was how I saw my turn in the witness stand.

I understood why it was important to come across genuine in court, but the thought of getting worked up in front of all those people left me frowning at Carolyn across the large meeting table, in disagreement with her enthusiasm for public displays of emotion.

I didn't want to get all snotty and shout things in court I would later regret. I was a self-confessed over-reactor, it was in my DNA along with my uninvited guest. I wasn't born with HIV but I did enter the world with a habit of over-reacting when under pressure. I was a breath-holder as a small child, a sure sign.

"There she goes again," my mum would think affectionately, as she watched me pass out in the garden from the kitchen window, while she did the dishes in the sink beneath it. It never worried her, she saw it coming, she knew the signs. Red face and stiff limbs before falling backwards like a two-foot plank of wood on the grass. Clonk. I fainted while quarrelling with other three-year-olds on a regular basis. Forgetting to breathe was easily done when getting into a state about something that at the time, mattered more.

Once I got started, I found it difficult to stop. Carolyn had no way of knowing it would be best all round if I stayed calm and centred because she didn't know me. Being an over-reactor wasn't easy. There should have been a support group for it. Over-reactors Anonymous.

After the trial, every newspaper article printed about the case included my attempt to slap Mark across the face on the day I'd confronted him in his shop. I had to explain my behaviour in court and the press loved it.

I grumbled about this to my son, Sam, because I liked

complaining about journalists.

"They could've used the trial as a platform for the better good of HIV awareness, but did they do that? Oh no, of course they didn't, because me clomping Mark one would sell their stupid papers. Okay, it was an act of violence which I'm not a fan of, but I only tried to hit him once which doesn't exactly make me The Bride in *Kill Bill*. I wasn't bouncing around the room in a yellow jumpsuit."

Sam hadn't seen the newspapers because he had been out of the area, thoroughly enjoying himself at university. My moaning on the phone had lead Sam to believe, I had jumped the barriers during the trial and tried to smack Mark in the mouth.

There was a pause in the conversation while Sam thought about this.

"Mum, can I just check I've got this right. You tried to hit Mark?" he eventually asked.

"Yes," I answered, wondering why he sounded so surprised.

"You actually tried to hit him?"

"Yeah! Too right I tried to hit him."

"Did the judge not try and stop you?"

"What has the judge got to do with it?"

"What have you done, Mum? Did the judge not try to stop you when you tried to hit Mark?"

"It was two years ago, in the shop. Why would the judge be in Mark's shop?"

This was the sort of thing that could happen when dealing with an over-reactor. Sam had thought, even for the briefest of moments, it wasn't out of the realms of possibility I had made a run for Mark across the courtroom and been tackled to the ground by security before being done for contempt of court.

I pressed Carolyn for a proper answer to my question because encouraging me to cry and get angry wasn't going to achieve anything, other than a visit from the court-appointed psychiatrist and a prescription for a course of diazepam.

Carolyn might not have been permitted to reveal what the defence had planned for me in his cross-examination. She may have been reluctant to say too much and risk frightening me with the reality of what it was going to be like once in the stand. Whatever her reasons, she still didn't say a great deal. Carolyn had at one time been a defence barrister, and not caring for it much because she enjoyed sleeping at night, had switched over to prosecuting those accused of breaking the law.

All Carolyn told me, was that her questions would be based on the content of all the police statements that were taken during the investigation. Her part in the proceedings sounded simple enough, she would be asking me in court to confirm the recorded facts were the truth.

"That's easy, I can do that," I replied while deciding for myself Mark's defence barrister was really going to be on my side too because the law was.

I was a good citizen who hadn't done anything wrong. The person I had in mind was another Linda, Joe or Carolyn, who would be my friend in court. If Carolyn noticed this, she kept it to herself, perhaps thinking my trusting ways would work in her favour.

This was the one and only time I saw Carolyn before the trial. As I watched her quickly gather up the files off the meeting table and rush off to wherever she was going next, I wondered to myself how some women managed to do the jobs they did.

Linda had a young family at home and it appeared Carolyn did too. When she turned to leave the room, I noticed a little pink hairband with a plastic Dora The Explorer button on it, holding her blonde hurriedly plaited hair in place.

47

The first day of the trial arrived, nearly two years on from the day I had walked into a police station to make my complaint.

Linda came to collect me. Anyone watching could easily have thought we were a pair of friends going off to do a day's shopping together. Little would indicate this was such a big day for both of us.

The significance of the day for Linda and myself as individuals was different, yet at the same time, the case had connected us. We had a mutual respect for one another's roles in the unusual circumstances that had brought us together.

I was particularly grateful for the little things, things that may have seemed trivial to others but mattered to me and were listened to. At the very beginning, I had asked Linda to make sure I was not referred to as a victim. The implication upset me. For my part, I had been anything but helpless and passive. Some might not have taken my request seriously but Linda did. She made sure, not one police officer ever forgot this small consideration.

Two years in, I didn't really care if the officers involved in my case knew my real name, but Linda and Joe did. They were so protective towards me, I got the impression even in meetings my courtroom alias, 'X', was used. I imagined Joe heading-up a meeting at the police station with a team of officers, pointing his finger to emphasise the seriousness of the matter while telling them, "Don't call 'X' the victim."

"Why, Serge?"

"She doesn't like it."

"But she is the victim in the case."

"Yes, we know that, but just don't do it. Refer to 'X' as the complainant. She doesn't mind that because it sounds proactive. Let's just keep her happy and all do as she says, shall we?"

"Can I just check I've got this right, Serge? We call her 'X', and we don't say the word 'victim' in front of her. Is that right? Is there anything else I need to know about her?"

"She's funny about rabbits. If you're taking a turn looking after her during the trial, don't mention anything to do with rabbits. I don't really understand it myself, but I once slipped up and said the kids kept a rabbit outside and she tore a strip of me, so she did. Look, it's simple. Do not say anything to upset her before she takes the stand. Okay?"

Sweet, they all were to me. But my firm favourites were Linda and Joe. It felt as if the two years investigating my complaint had become more than just earning a salary to them. My story moved people, I could see that, and it meant a lot.

We arrived at the court building and Linda parked up, in the same quiet spot she had used on our look-see visit. It was to the side of the building and nothing more than a gravelly grass verge. Linda pulled a homemade cardboard sign out of her handbag with 'OFFICIAL POLICE BUSINESS' written on it in green felt-tip and wedged it upright against her windscreen using an empty Coke can as a stopper. On the other side of the sign was a picture of a cartoon toucan. I envisaged Linda scrambling around that morning for something to write on before leaving to pick me up, Fruit Loops spilling all over her kitchen table and rolling off it onto the floor.

"Give me a ticket if they dare," she laughed. "I need to get 'X' into court. Let's see if they argue with that."

There was a side entrance to the building, an inconspicuous door, used mostly to avoid press photographers and other people who had reason to be at the various trials taking place inside. Linda told me photographers were already waiting at the front of the building, which was usual in cases that had generated high levels of interest.

The door led directly to an area in the building referred to by the police as the victim suite. It was completely sectioned off from the rest of the building and accessible only to people who had permission to be in it.

Linda spoke to someone through the intercom system on the wall, announcing our arrival, and the side door was buzzed open by the court official on the other side of it. The woman explained apologetically the necessity to make sure I didn't have any illegal drugs or weapons in my possession and after patting me down under my coat, asked for my handbag.

The search for weapons, I could understand. Some witnesses might have viewed court as their last chance to gun down a defendant, but the illegal drugs part was a mystery to me.

Why would a witness do drugs in a building full of law enforcement officers? I thought as I watched the woman empty the contents of my handbag onto her desk. To my mind, if someone wanted to get fucked up on illegal substances on the day they were required to give evidence in court, it would have been far more sensible to do it at home before they got there.

Linda and I signed our names in a big book on the desk and I was handed my bag back after the few items I had in it, were placed back inside. Along with my purse and phone, these were a book, a tuna sandwich, a packet of cheesy Wotsits and the prescription bottle of my medication I took everywhere with me.

Alex had done a good job on me. I had latched onto my bottles of tablets like my life quite literally depended on them and was never without one to hand. If I got kidnapped and held prisoner in a lunatic's garden shed as a sex-slave, I had nothing to worry about. I had a month's worth of HIV medication on me at all times. The court official didn't mention the bottle or enquire what the tablets were rattling around inside of it. I had a feeling she already knew.

As Linda and I made our way up a flight of stairs to a set of electric double doors at the top of them, I heard the court official say to someone on the phone, "She's on her way."

The glass doors at the top of the stairs opened instantly as I stepped up to them. There was a gathering of people on the other side of the doors, police officers, and others who worked in the building in various roles. I could physically feel their curiosity. Some of them couldn't hide expressions of surprise or relief I was there. I had made it. I was in the building and had not stood them up. Linda had not been turned away at my front door by me standing in my pyjamas, bottom lip trembling, too frightened to go through with the events of the day and no intention of going anywhere.

There was a plan for the day already in place. I would take the stand first to give evidence as soon as everything was ready. Several things needed to be taken care of before this could happen, so another part of the plan was to make sure I was never left alone. This was a kind but unnecessary gesture. I felt so nervous all I wanted to do was sit quietly on my own until it was time and the judge was ready for me.

Linda was running around the building with a list of things to do, so in her place, other officers took it in turns to look after me. They tried awkwardly to make conversation which would tail off to nothingness. I appreciated their efforts, but this was not a morning I could manage to do polite small talk.

A Victim Support Volunteer even had a crack at me but gave up after a while, patting me on the shoulder as she left.

"I can see you want to be on your own, dear, but give me a wave if you need anything, a cup of tea or a chat. I've brought a 'Bella' in with me to read if it gets quiet, but you can have it, if it helps take your mind off things."

Everyone was being too nice. I started to get that horrible feeling of tearfulness when other people were too kind and I needed to avoid it. If 'X' got upset this early on, there would be way too much fretting over me, police officers rushing around and bumping into each other while trying to figure out how to stop the waterworks.

"Good God! She's crying! What are we going to do? Quick! Let's all make a massive fuss over her and make her feel even more self-conscious than she already does, that'll do the trick!"

Linda came back to the victim suite to check on me and tell me Mark had also arrived.

"Where is he?" I asked her.

"Don't worry, you won't see him. He is in another part of the building, a waiting area where the defendants are kept. It is set up that way on purpose," Linda replied.

Mark, in the cowardy custard suite, was at the same time receiving the news that I was also in the building.

"We've just got to wait now. Mark will be given one last chance to change his plea. The good news is, now that he knows you're here, his legal representative is encouraging him to do so. The sensible thing for Mark to do now is plead 'guilty'. I think there's a good chance he will," Linda said before leaving again.

Later into the morning, Linda waved to me from the doorway of the large communal waiting room I was in, beckoning me to come out into the corridor with her so we could talk in private. We found an alcove to stand in and with heads bowed together we whispered to each other, discussing the information she had just received.

"Mark is not going to change his plea," she told me.

"Against advice?" I asked.

"It looks that way. I get the impression the last thing his legal representative wants is for this case to go to trial. HIV transmission cases are his thing, he's never lost one, but it's Mark's choice at the end of the day."

"So, the trial will start today?"

"Yes. The other thing I have to tell you is, Mark will not be taking the stand."

"He can make that decision?"

"It was probably the advice he was given, which he took this time. Mark wouldn't be doing himself any favours by taking the stand. His legal representative will now become his defence barrister in court and plead his case for him."

"What is his defence going to be?"

"He's going down the route of denial."

My opinion on Mark changing his plea had always been split right down the middle. The evidence against him was stacked up high but his attitude hadn't changed. Evidence versus attitude. In the run-up to the trial date, I could never quite decide which one would outweigh the other.

I had been sure Mark would leave it as late as possible but sticking with his 'not guilty' plea was going some. If a verdict of 'guilty' was reached by the jury at the end of the trial, he could receive the maximum prison sentence with no negotiation for a reduction.

Mark's decision to go ahead with a trial, could only mean he was hanging out in the hope I was unable to cope and break down in the stand, would refuse to cooperate with questioning, or got so confused I said something that would vindicate him of what he was being accused of.

"What's he like? The defence barrister?" I asked, suddenly curious because I was now going to meet him.

"He seems like a reasonable person. Quietly spoken, actually. Not someone I would have put down as a barrister on meeting him, had it been under different circumstances," Linda replied.

"That's good, right?"

"Definitely. I was surprised at how easy he was to talk to."

Linda looked at her watch as she spoke. "Let's get on with it and at least your bit will be over today. I need to get back to the judge and let him know what's going on, he has asked for your final response regarding the proceedings. Are you willing to take the stand and give evidence now that we know Mark is not going to change his plea?"

"Yes," I replied.

Back in the waiting room, morning turned into afternoon. I stared at the clock on the wall, the second-hand tick-tocking around it in never-ending circles. I couldn't look at my book or eat anything. I thought of myself at home that morning, preparing for the day and thinking I might get bored or hungry. The atmosphere in the place was charged. The waiting filled my thoughts with what was going to happen next and the stress knot in my stomach left no room for food. Eventually, Linda re-appeared.

"The judge has found something in the casefile he doesn't like. That's what the hold-up is," she told me.

"What is it?" I asked.

"The absence of an HIV test result from one of your ex-partners, someone from years ago and we've got to find him. Now."

"Why? I thought we'd finished with all of that?"

"So did I, but the judge doesn't want to leave anything to chance. He wants a negative test result from him and isn't prepared to go ahead until he's got it."

One of the boyfriends I had told Linda about had not gone to Eve for a test because Linda and I had decided it wasn't necessary. His name was still on the witness statement the judge had read because Linda had recorded him as an ex-partner.

"It has been such a long time, how are we supposed to find him that quickly and what happens if we can't?" I asked Linda.

"The judge will postpone the trial. It could be weeks before another date is available in court. We've got to try and find him."

48

I hadn't given erectile dysfunction much thought until I met Jonathan.

When we were together in the same room with no clothes on it was a high-stress environment for him. When Jonathan looked at me naked, Gracie Fields could be heard singing in the background, *Wish Me Luck as You Wave Me Goodbye*.

Most of the time, I didn't want to upset Jonathan's penis any more than I had already, so I would suggest putting our clothes back on and having a nice cup of tea and a slice of Battenberg instead. It was all very tiring and I used to get hungry.

Jonathan was a decent person, gentle and sensitive, and I didn't want to insult his manhood by not including him on the ex-boyfriend list because it made me feel bad, even though I wasn't sure whether he counted or not. It was a grey area, what all that stressful fumbling around meant, and I had tried to be as accurate as I could in all the information I had given to Linda and Joe.

I had told Linda, I wasn't confident what we did together was sex because my vagina terrified him. I now wished I hadn't bothered mentioning Jonathan in the first place because the judge now wanted him sent to Eve for an HIV test. Today. It was my own mini vaginagate.

I was all out of ideas on how the police could contact Jonathan. I hadn't seen or heard of him in years. I wasn't even sure what name he went by, his birth name, or the surname given to him by his adoptive parents. Jonathan had had a rough time of it as a child. Through the care system and in and out of foster homes, he had eventually been adopted. I couldn't be sure what name he preferred to use and had no idea where he lived.

Finding Jonathan, getting him to take an HIV test and the results collected by Linda to give to the judge, had to be done quicker than you could say "flaccid". Otherwise, the trial would be postponed.

It was a long shot, but Joe rushed off to look at the database at the police station and rushed back just as quick with a printout in his hand. Joe held up the mugshot in front of me and when I looked at the picture it was Jonathan, a lot older, but definitely him.

Jonathan had gotten into an argument with a police officer after getting very drunk on the night of the day, he had caught his wife cheating on him with a firefighter. Not quite the same division of uniformed services, but the police officer's presence had still been enough to tip him over the edge of reason and vent his uncharacteristic anger. When the officer had approached Jonathan, and told him to quieten down and go home, Jonathan had thrown a kebab at him.

I could see from the photograph this was the case. The contents of a doner kebab were imprinted on the front of the white shirt Jonathan had worn to work that day. He had returned home earlier than usual and found his wife in bed with a fireman. It was a distressing sight, his wife riding the fireman like a bucking bronco.

"I'll slide up and down your pole any time you like," she had said in free abandon as Jonathan walked in the room, the fireman's firefighting hat bobbing about on the top half of her head which under different circumstances, would have looked cute.

The chilli sauce and red cabbage stains on the front of Jonathan's shirt had come about on the evening in question when the officer of the law had pinned him to the ground. Jonathan had landed on top of the weapon he had attacked the police officer with, which was his kebab.

This had been necessary because Jonathan refused to leave the kebab shop, which was called 'Shish Happens', stating it was the closest thing he had to a home. He had then wrestled with the officer while shouting at the top of his voice, "You're all just a bunch of cocks! Handcuff if you can, Po-Po, I am not leaving without a fight! I've had enough of being Mr. Nice!"

Thirty seconds later, handcuffed and in the back of a police car, Jonathan had broken down about his wife and sobbed uncontrollably. He told the police officer how sorry he was about the kebab but it didn't make any difference. Jonathan had really pissed him off and the officer arrested him anyway.

Three hours after identifying Jonathan in the picture Joe had shown me, he was sitting with Eve in the clinic.

"Please tell her from me, I wish her the best of luck, whoever she is," he had said, as Eve took his blood sample.

49

Thanks to Jonathan's kebab and his rap sheet because of it, the trial still went ahead albeit a day late.

Second time around, the court building wasn't so overwhelming. Instead of the main waiting room in the victim suite, I was offered a room of my own to sit in. It was a small play area tucked away from the busy central corridor, used for video linking evidence from young children to a courtroom. I imagined them busily involved in their play, innocently oblivious of being part of a legal process, as they acted out situations using dolls or drew pictures with crayons for a therapist.

I felt comfortable in the little room, the things in it familiar because of the children I worked with. I walked around it, looking at the toys and games on the shelves. Picking up a book I had read out loud to eager little listeners hundreds of times, I flicked through the pages of *The Tiger Who Came to Tea*. I didn't read the words, I knew them off by heart. I was grateful for the quietness and privacy the room gave me. The thought of having a pretend tea party at the little yellow table with a police officer, or squabbling over whose turn it was next with the Fuzzy Felt farm animal set, cheered me up.

Unlike the day before, I didn't have long to wait before Linda appeared at the door of the playroom and told me the judge was ready for me in court. I told Linda and Joe not to worry about me and smiled back at them, as they both gave me a nervous little wave from the end of the corridor. They looked like anxious parents standing at the gates on the first day of big school.

One of the Victim Support Volunteers escorted me back through the victim suite and into the lift that took us up to the floor where the courtrooms were located. The courtrooms were all in a row at the front of the building. Each one had a seated waiting area directly in front of it. Anyone who had a desire or reason to see the coming and going of people involved in the various trials that took place in the courtrooms, could use these public areas for as long as necessary. I remembered the open layout of the building from the day Linda and I had looked around on our pre-trial visit. It had worried me then, the thought of those waiting areas full of people.

This was not something I had to worry about anymore. I was impressed with the effort that had gone into making sure my walk to the courtroom was free of an interested audience. True to his word, the judge had arranged screening all the way through the building, right up to the witness stand, so not a single soul could get a glimpse of me. The screens were on wheels, secured together by cable ties around each set of metal poles, to stop any chancers taking a lucky peek.

When we reached the courtroom door it was immediately opened for me by the security guard standing in front of it. "Good luck," my escort said, as she handed me over to a woman on the other side of the door.

The witness stand was only a few paces away from the door so witnesses could enter and exit the courtroom as easily as possible. After I was sworn in, the room went quiet. I suddenly became conscious of being in the same room as Mark. It was a strange feeling, knowing he was there, on the other side of a screen to my left. He could hear everything I said but he couldn't see me. He wasn't allowed to.

From where I was standing, I could see the judge to my right, his chair on a platform that made him higher up than everyone else in the room. Opposite the judge was a row of desks. Carolyn was standing behind the one nearest to me and at the other end, a man sat silently, working away on his laptop without looking up. Directly opposite where I stood was the jury box with twelve seats in it, all taken.

Even though all the people in the room were in reasonably close proximity to each other, including me, the formality still made the atmosphere extremely tense. An uncomfortable tightness in my throat made it difficult to swallow. I tried to disguise how vulnerable I felt by keeping my chin up to avoid the temptation to stare at my feet.

You have every right to be here today, don't be scared, these people are on your side, I told myself.

Linda wasn't allowed in the courtroom with me, no one was. The public gallery was empty because that was what I had asked for. I hadn't even let Livvy, or friends who had offered, come with me and wait in the victim suite. I didn't want to have to worry about other people worrying about me. All I wanted was to get on with it, without any distractions.

I hadn't expected the civility of introductions, but it was still unsettling being the centre of attention and yet everyone in the room behaving as if I wasn't there. The only person I knew was Carolyn. The man at the far end of the row of desks and closest to the jurors, who I assumed was Mark's barrister, didn't speak or look up from his laptop until it was his turn to ask me questions.

Carolyn was talking to the judge. She broke off from the

conversation for a brief moment to catch my eye and silently mouth, "You okay?" to which I replied with a solemn nod.

Most unnerving of all was the twelve pairs of eyes on me, mentally detailing everything they could see. When I looked back at the jurors and smiled shyly, some turned away awkwardly, embarrassed at being caught out staring.

The judge instructed Carolyn to begin. In her opening statement, Carolyn told the jury what they were going to hear and what their job would be at the end of the proceedings. The jurors' eyes followed Carolyn's when she turned to me and smiled. She asked some warm-up questions. How old I was, how many children I had, the nature of my employment. Normal things to ease me in. Carolyn wanted me to talk about myself, she wanted the jurors to like me.

After a pause, alerting me to the impending change in her questions, Carolyn gently asked, "What was your first thought when you found out you were HIV-positive?"

I looked at the jurors when I gave my answer to the question. "How am I going to tell my children I am going to die because I have AIDS?"

The first of the women covered her mouth with her hand when she started to cry. She glanced at the woman sitting next to her, who was shaking her head from side to side with her eyes closed as if it was too uncomfortable to look at me.

Mothers, imagining having to tell their own children something so horrendous, I thought, as I watched them.

The rest of Carolyn's questions were not meant to evoke a strong reaction from the jury, it wasn't necessary, her first question had been enough. She asked me to confirm chronologically the order of events recorded in police statements, the nature of my relationship with

Mark and the lack of any indication of his HIV status.

Next, Carolyn made the jury aware she was going to present a list of names that would be referred to in court by an allocated initial only, making sure they all noted it was evidence that had been provided to the defence. Carolyn was going to beat the defence barrister to it, by addressing the people on the list first.

Clever, I thought. *She's trumped him.*

With a copy of the names and initials in front of me, Carolyn asked me to describe my involvement with each of the individuals. Even though she already knew what my responses were going to be, Carolyn still couldn't help smiling at the jurors' reactions, as they struggled to hide their amusement at some of my explanations. After the last person had been discussed, Carolyn asked me to state where the list had originated from and its intended purpose, before addressing the jury directly.

"This woman's life has been pulled apart in the last two years. If it wasn't devastating enough that she found out she was HIV-positive, she then received the news it could have been avoided, had the man she loved and trusted simply told her the truth. Then the harassment started, threats to reveal her identity and HIV status."

Carolyn paused, using the silence to her advantage. The jurors waited in readiness for her to continue.

"Can any of us in this room honestly say, we can even begin to imagine how that must have felt for her? She is still here today though, standing in front of you all and I hope you agree, her presence says just as much as the testimonies you are going to hear throughout the course of the proceedings."

By the time Carolyn's questioning drew to a close, the jurors were aware no HIV test results of any past partners were positive other than Mark's, the significance of seroconversion, and my unwillingness to accept Mark knew he was HIV-positive before he met me.

Carolyn's final question pre-empted the direction the defence would take. She deliberately made it sound recriminatory and it worked, effective because it came from her.

"Are you looking for someone to blame for your HIV status?"

I responded in genuine exasperation, "Why would anyone want the endurance test my life has become in the last two years? And it's not just me, my children have had to live it too. My teenage daughter got asked in high school one day, if her mother had given anybody else AIDS. Imagine that?"

I drew a deep breath and slowly exhaled before continuing.

"No, this is not about blame. I am doing my best to put my life back together. I didn't ask for this chaos in my life. I could have died. I am angry, with every right to be, but I am not bitter. I feel lucky to be alive."

I looked around the room at all the faces. "What was I supposed to do? Nothing? Leave him to destroy someone else's life?"

"Is it possible the defendant was unaware of the damage his actions could do? In denial of his own diagnosis of HIV?" Carolyn asked.

"No."

"Why?"

"Because denial involves feelings of loss and helplessness. Narcissism, on the other hand, is driven by vanity and greed."

"And you believe the defendant to be a narcissist?"

"Mark knew he was HIV-positive and concealed it because of vanity. He took what he wanted out of greed. That's what I believe. Can I be honest with you?" I said to Carolyn.

"Go ahead, that's what you're here for," Carolyn prompted.

"If Mark is basing his defence on denial, then that makes me feel sick. Sick to the stomach. I've seen denial on the faces of parents I've work with. Parents, who are going to lose their baby to some dreadful disease, or because of being born with a heart that doesn't work. I've witnessed that level of pain. People in true denial don't know how to live if the worst happens. They don't think they'll survive it."

I turned to the jurors and said angrily, "They do not, drive around in sports cars, spend a lot of money on clothes and holidays, and have unprotected sex with whoever they want."

I turned back to Carolyn. "Sorry. It just makes me feel so mad."

"Don't be. You have every right," Carolyn said.

The defence barrister didn't look at me when he asked his first question. He kept his eyes on his laptop, hands either side of it, as he stood up from his chair and leant over it.

This won't take long, I thought to myself, pleased with the way things were going.

I had reached this conclusion because I couldn't see what was left to ask that hadn't already been covered by Carolyn. Nevertheless, the defence had to take his turn and his cross-examination began.

Shit, I thought, when his questions started. *Shit, shit, shit.*

My assumption that the defence barrister would really be on my side, and we were all just going to pretend he was there for Mark, had been wrong. If this was the nice, quietly spoken man Linda had described to me, being a defence barrister was a role he played and he played it well.

It started out a drip, a trickle of doubt, that this was not going to be easy or over soon. The realisation I was losing control picked up pace, the flow of apprehension becoming waves of panic that I couldn't stop.

I had never been good at remembering numbers off the top of my head. Whether they were telephone numbers or dates, they all had to be written down if important. Names I was okay with, but numbers, there was not a chance I'd recall a sequence of them correctly relying on memory alone.

The initials next to the names on the list were a problem too, even though the cross-referencing had been at my request. I had asked the judge in my Victim Impact Statement to keep all names anonymous in court because of the press. I was 'X', and in turn, someone else was 'A', another 'B', and so on. No relevance to their actual names, simply labelled alphabetically from top to bottom, in the same order the list had originally been written.

The defence barristers' questions were regarding the list, leaving out the silly stuff he didn't want the jurors reminded of. I was asked to provide him with the dates of when relationships started and ended, going back over twenty years, but purposely not in any order. An initial would be stated, followed by a demand for the dates that matched up with the person.

I knew all the dates, from my very first relationship to my last. I'd gone over them with Linda and written them down in a police statement, but I couldn't recite them from memory quick enough for him. The initials slowed down my responses because I was doing three things at once. Listening to the questions, cross-referencing and sums.

When I looked down at the piece of paper in front of me, first I had to find the name that matched the initial, then try to work out the maths in my head. How old I was when the relationship started and what year that would make it. While I was thinking about this, another question would be impatiently asked, breaking my concentration.

The names and letters on the list began to look blurry. I couldn't keep up and my mind went blank. Mark's barrister was doing an excellent job of making it look like I hadn't the slightest idea who, or how many, people I had slept with. If I asked for clarification, I was ignored, or told I wasn't there to do the asking.

"Well? When were you in a relationship with this person?"

"Which one? I don't know who you are talking about."

"No, you don't, do you?"

"What I meant was, who are you referring to?"

"You are not here to ask the questions. If you, don't know who you've had sex with, then that is all the court needs to know."

The initials were a problem for two reasons. They sounded clinical to the jury and complicated answering the questions, making it easier to trip me up. To my horror, I could feel the prickling of tears on their way. I was getting upset and everyone in the room knew it. I needed help and spoke directly to the judge, even though I was unsure if this was allowed.

"Your Honour, I am sorry, I want to answer the questions but I'm getting confused. I can't organise my thoughts properly."

I looked in the direction of the defence barrister then back at the judge. "He's doing it on purpose," I said to him in a low voice, as if telling him something he didn't already know.

I half expected a reprimand from the judge and this was a risk I was prepared to take. It was a relief when the judge spoke. He had no intention of making me feel even worse than I already did.

"Would thirty minutes on your own to gather your thoughts help?"

"Yes, Your Honour, it would. That would help a lot."

"I can't let you take the list with you, but would some paper to write on help you work out the dates?"

"Yes, that would help too."

"Right then," the judge said firmly. "You will be escorted to a quiet area. I will allow half an hour for an interval. You must make sure you do not speak to anyone during it. Do you agree to this?"

"Yes, I won't speak to anyone."

"Court adjourned for thirty minutes. I want everyone back here by twelve midday."

The judge held up a piece of paper and a pen, asking the court official who had sworn me in, to pass them over to me. I nodded to him in silent appreciation, grateful to be let out of the room. I was going to cry, holding it in was giving me a headache and I needed to get out quickly because I didn't want anyone to see me upset. I didn't want pity. The courtroom door was held open for me to leave and once out in the corridor, I was escorted back to the victim suite.

Linda and Joe were still in the corridor waiting for me. Their faces lit up, delighted I was back and thinking it was all over. Seeing them started me off, hot tears rolled down my cheeks as I waved them away, telling them not to come near me because I wasn't allowed to talk to anyone.

Joe still sitting on a chair, put his elbows on his knees and head in his hands, and stared at the linoleum covered floor between his shoes. Linda had stood up to greet me. She stayed put, stock-still and open-mouthed, as I rushed past them both.

On my own in the playroom, I gulped down air and sobbed at the same time. All I wanted to do was leave, go home, and never set foot in the building ever again. I felt humiliated. I didn't want to go back, dreading the thought of having to face him again.

Him? I thought to myself. *Which 'him' has brought my life to this point?*

It wasn't the one behind the desk, he was just earning a living to pay his mortgage like the rest of us. It was the one behind the glass wall at the back of the courtroom.

In the quiet of the little haven of a room I was in, I started to calm down and think rationally. The desired result was being achieved and I was losing.

It can't end like this, I thought. *I won't let it.*

Now I understood the rules, I started to feel angry again, the familiar sensation replacing the tears of humiliation. A smouldering heat rose inside me as I thought about the morning. Mark would have been delighted when I left the courtroom. If I didn't return that would be the end of it, he would be free to go and publicly brand me with whatever insult he saw fit.

The judge had decided on an early lunch break for the jurors and this gave me another hour to get even more angry, about the whole thing. Every single bit of it. I had been hurt by Mark in so many ways and by insisting on a trial, he was still doing it.

If I walked out, leaving my self-respect behind at the victim suite door, nothing had changed.

50

I had done some stupendously stupid things in my life.

I once managed to lock myself in my friends flat for a day. In the lobby she shared with her downstairs neighbour, to be exact. I pulled the door behind me having stayed the night to drink wine and her neighbour had double locked the front door. I didn't have a key to get back in, forgot my phone and had no food or water on me because I'd been on my way to the gym. It was a long day. I had to pee in my sports bag. I was stuck in that hot hell hole, hungover, for nine hours until my friend returned from work. She found me asleep on her doormat in a foetal position, so dehydrated my lips had curled in on themselves and were stuck to my teeth.

Me and my toaster were the reason why an enormous hotel on Brighton seafront had to be evacuated one sunny weekend. I was there for a hen party and preferring to be on my own first thing in the morning, had brought a toaster with me for the bagel I liked with coffee for breakfast. It never occurred to me, it would set the fire alarms off. I threw the toaster out the window, smashing it to bits on the pavement it hit, then sashayed past the firemen in the lobby as if the whole debacle had nothing to do with me. I hadn't had time to put a pair of knickers on, let alone make up, so wearing sunglasses and swinging a handbag nonchalantly with the incriminating packet of bagels in it, I walked out of the building. One of the firemen winked at me. I ignored him and kept on walking. Once out of sight, I hurled the bag of bagels backwards over my shoulder and legged it.

I stole a neighbour's rabbit. Technically it wasn't theft because he was in my garden. Stuck in a cage all the time, on his own, bitten to bits by insects and terrorised at night by cats and foxes, I helped him escape. By opening the door to his prison and shooing him into my garden. I was allergic to all things fluffy, but it was too late. I'd bonded, it was a done deal. He lived in my house with me. I potty trained him to poop and pee in a litter box, so he could go anywhere he liked but the only place he wanted to be, was with me. He was a people rabbit. For the next eight years, I woke up to a rabbit licking my forehead, coughed up furballs and sneezed myself stupid. I fucking loved my rabbit and cried for a month after he'd died.

As a young person, I went to work on a summer camp in the state of Vermont in North America for eight weeks and didn't come back. For two years anyway. I missed my flight on purpose and had no money. I bummed a ride to Miami, got a job waitressing and made friends who I lived with. When my visa ran out, I didn't care. I stayed in America illegally and as an illegal alien, I could have gone to prison if caught. When I left the country, I boarded the aircraft using someone else's boarding pass, which was unbelievably possible back then. If that plane had crashed, no one would have known who I was. No record of me ever leaving the states, I would have simply disappeared. Spooky as fuck.

I had been to the United States of America one other time in my life. I got married in Las Vegas to someone I didn't know that well who turned out not to be a very nice person. I suggested putting it on hold the week before the holiday and he threatened to leave me. Curveballed, I married him. The ceremony took place in a drive-through wedding facility by an ordained Elvis impersonator. After all, it was Vegas. As soon as we hit English soil, I knew I'd made a mistake and divorced him a year later.

I got engaged, a lot. Flattered and rushing in as usual, I'd agree to a proposal of marriage and within no time at all, the commitment-phobe in me would be working out an exit plan. I had a lot of wedding and engagement rings knocking about. Livvy used to play with them. I fished them all out of the bottom of her dressing-up box one day and flogged the lot at a local pawnbroker. I used the money to go to Tenerife with Gorgeous Gary for a week. I could have put it to far better use at home, but it was the only way I could afford the holiday and I thought it would cement our relationship. It didn't do anything of the kind. He dumped me a month later.

I moved in and out of houses, a lot. Maybe I just did everything, a lot. I should have been a traveller, a caravan would have been so much easier and the not staying in one place too long thing would've worked for me. Once in a new house, two years and I'd be off again. No sooner finished decorating somewhere and it would be on the market. Perhaps I was always searching for something I couldn't find, the same of which could have been said, about relationships.

I terminated an unplanned pregnancy. Already a mother, I convinced myself afterwards that I had killed my own child and tortured myself for years. I ended the relationship I was in because I couldn't bear to look at him and the baby chase years, as I would come to think of them, ensued. I made a lot of bad relationship choices because of them. In my desperation to feel better, I thought if I met someone who could give me a replacement baby, I could pour all my love into that child and make everything right. It was the guilt I couldn't get past. This was a stupid yet totally forgivable way to think; the basis for a healthy relationship, it was not. I never had a relationship again that lasted long enough to even consider having a child with someone.

I'd had unprotected sex at times over the years. Every time I had, I thought it would be the last. Then something would go wrong and it would end, and I would move on. I was good at endings. I didn't understand people who weren't.

I'd done some stupid things in my life, I wasn't denying it.

But I did not, deserve this.

51

I had entered a game. I hadn't known it at the start of the day but I did now.

A trial was a strategic competition. The opponents in the game, battled for supremacy by refusing to change their own aim in the hope their challenger would weaken first.

It had to be viewed that way and the sooner the penny dropped for the witness in court, the better. If complainants seeking justice took the process personally, they would lose. Legal professionals were paid to ensure a victory for their client and the most skilful of which, would manage to convince the witness in the stand it was personal. Anything within their power would be used to destroy their victim and avoid a defeat. It was called discrediting the witness and Mark's barrister had got to it from his very first question.

It had taken me a while to catch up but now, I understood.

The quality of the testimony provided by the witness was what proved guilt beyond reasonable doubt. The aim of the defence was to demonstrate to the jury I was an unreliable witness, unworthy of their trust. The defence could use personal information that had been made available to him, either by his client or another source and just about anything was fair game. I would be presented as disreputable and dishonest as possible. It was one big show for an audience, the jurors, and the show was called the Test of Believability.

The person given the task of representing Mark did not know me or wish to. I was a pay cheque, not a person. He was an employed professional, trained in emotional detachment, and it was what he did best. Belligerence was not only acceptable in court, it was a given.

Back in the witness stand, not that I looked it as I pleasantly declined the offer of a seat and a box of tissues from the judge, I was seething. I stood up straight, where I would remain for the next four hours and kept my eyes on my opponent, even though he did not look back at me unless he had to. I forgot that Mark was even in the room.

The boyfriend list, old hat by now, was still current as far as the opponent was concerned. This repetition was tedious but purposeful. The opponent needed me to feel as uncomfortable as possible and asking me questions about my past sex life was the way he was going to do it. The names and dates, now in front of me having written them down in the interval, were also a prelude to other questions and subjects, building blocks in the humiliation parade.

The opponent might have known a lot of things about me but he didn't know everything. He didn't know about my stubbornness, that once my mind was made up about something, I didn't budge. Like a limpet on a rock, that was me, a little steadfast limpet.

I cooperated, I had to, but my style which I couldn't change, looked like it drove the opponent mad. Me being me irritated him to death.

The opponent wanted to talk about sex but I didn't. I wasn't in the mood. I couldn't have been coaxed into it even if the opponent's technique had included verbal foreplay, which it didn't.

"What kind of relationship did you have with this person?" the opponent asked about one of the people on the list.

"We spent some time together, over a few months or so," I answered, uncertain what else to say about Jonathan.

"Were you in a relationship with him?"

"Of a fashion."

"It is an easy enough question. Did you have a physical relationship with him?"

"We held hands sometimes."

"What else did you do with him?"

"We had a nice day out in York once. Visited the castle. Mind it poured down, rained cats and dogs, it did."

"Did you have sexual intercourse with this person or not?"

"He had issues."

"And what is that supposed to mean?"

"Difficult childhood."

The judge helped me out, looking at me over the top of his glasses.

"Are you trying to say this person couldn't achieve an erection?"

"Thank you, Your Honour. Yes, Your Honour. I believe that is the word I was looking for."

Jonathan's erectile dysfunction had got a shout-out in court. It wasn't meant to be funny but the women in the jury box could barely contain themselves.

Eventually, the opponent's questions came around to Mark.

"Did the defendant rape you?"

"No."

"Then why did you state in a conversation with your health

advisor he had?"

"I didn't."

"I have details of the conversation here in front of me, taken from your client contact record at the clinic. You stated you felt like you'd been raped."

"That's correct, I did say that. It was how I felt when I found out."

"Therefore, you were lying. The defendant didn't rape you."

"Eve called me a few days after the meeting to ask how I was feeling, so I told her. It was a private conversation, I was unaware it was going to be recorded."

"You admit it then, you wrongfully accused the defendant of rape because you were angry."

"That word does not appear anywhere in any of the statements I made to the police. Mark was charged with Grievous Bodily Harm. He abused me. He assaulted me and used sex to do it. 'Rape' might not have been an appropriate word to use, but because of the devastation his actions had caused me, it was the one that sprang to mind."

All questions were closed with no introduction on purpose. A pause while the opponent read his notes from his laptop was the only indicator of a change in direction.

"Do you know how many sexual partners the defendant had before meeting you?"

"No."

"Why not?"

"It never came up in conversation and I didn't ask."

"Why not?"

"I knew he'd had other relationships, of course he had. I don't think I have ever asked anyone how many people they've slept with, it would be rude."

"Yet, you knew he had a reputation."

"He was liked by women and gossiped about, just like lots of other single people in my town. I'm gossiped about, it's not nice, so I tend not to get involved when it's done to another person. I knew Mark was capable of longevity in his relationships, he had been in two that he told me about, that had lasted years."

"Wasn't it said that the defendant had lots of different partners and little integrity when it came to his sexual relationships?"

"I don't know, and even if I did, I'm not sure how comfortable I'd be repeating gossip in a court of law. I don't mean to tell you how to do your job, but why are you asking me what other people have said about Mark? Isn't that hearsay? How would I know what was factually accurate, unless I had seen or heard it for myself?"

It was a balancing act to come across self-assertive but not a smart Alec, especially when provoked. It wasn't my intention to sound facetious but sometimes it was unavoidable. There was no mistaking how much it annoyed the opponent when this happened.

"You take no responsibility, do you? For the situation, you have found yourself in. Do you not think, it would have been sensible to ask such questions during your relationship with the defendant and before you consented to unprotected sex?"

"I consented to what I thought was a loving and safe relationship. Not to be HIV-positive."

"Did you ever discuss HIV or sexual health screening with the defendant? Did you take any measures to protect yourself at all? No, you didn't and now, you are looking for someone to blame."

There it was again. The big, bad 'blame' theory. Carolyn had been right to anticipate it would be included in Mark's defence and even though she had already covered it, the opponent couldn't resist using it again.

In a wave of frustration and anger, I replied equally as loudly, "No I didn't, and I agree with you, that makes me very stupid. But it wouldn't have made any difference if I had asked Mark about testing and HIV because he would have lied. I would still be HIV-positive because your client is an accomplished liar."

I took a moment to compose myself, before finishing what I wanted to say. "Not asking those very sensible questions might make me stupid, but it doesn't make your client any less guilty of the crime he has been charged with. Mark knew he could be prosecuted if he infected me with HIV and it was a risk he was prepared to take, along with my safety."

If a line of questioning looked like it was working in the favour of the prosecution, it was dropped instantly and replaced by another. I was required to give a response to all questions. That was the deal I had agreed to, along with handing over my medical records to the defence.

"I see from your medical record you've had a pregnancy terminated. Is that correct?"

I ignored the opponent and looked at Carolyn for help. "Is he allowed to do this? Can't you object? Stop him?" I asked her.

All Carolyn said was one word. "Sorry."

The opponent was furious. He shouted angrily at me, "You will answer anything I see fit to ask you! How dare you question my authority!"

The judge looked up sharply and stopped him from saying any more. "You need to lower your voice. There is no need to talk to the witness like that, I won't allow it." Then looking at me, the judge continued speaking. "But you do need to answer the question. You gave your consent to your medical records being examined by the defence."

Shook up but still standing, I nodded to the judge before looking back at the opponent to answer his question.

"Yes. That is correct."

"And yet, after this, you tried to conceive again having aborted a healthy foetus."

"When?"

"You don't remember having an abortion then changing your mind and trying to conceive again?"

"Of course I remember having the termination. I believed at the time failed contraception was not a reason to have a child, but that didn't stop me from feeling terribly depressed afterwards. As you can see from my medical records, I took medication for the depression for months. It was a decision I did not take lightly and an awful time in my life, but I don't know what you mean about trying to get pregnant again."

"You saw your doctor because you thought you might be experiencing a miscarriage. Remember that?"

"I remember going to see my doctor one time because I had an abdominal pain, my period was late, and both these things worried me. He must have recorded the reason for my visit being a possible pregnancy or miscarriage. It was a long time ago, but I vaguely remember it being discussed."

"Because you were trying to conceive."

"No. I wasn't. Failed contraception had already happened once. For some time afterwards, I was overly worried it might happen again, even though it never did. I was not planning on having a child with the person I was with at the time. I'd married him for all the wrong reasons and knew it wasn't going to last."

I wrapped my fingers around the wooden edge of the witness box and stared at the opponent icily. "Sorry, if that isn't the answer you were looking for. It took me a long time to forgive myself for having an abortion and having to talk about it, here, is very difficult."

The opponent did not react in any way. Continuing to study the notes on his laptop, he asked, "Are you saying you weren't pregnant when you went to see the doctor?"

"Can you see anything in my medical records, such as a positive pregnancy test, that suggests I was?" I replied.

I thought he had finished but the opponent pressed on, confident he had something worth pursuing.

"You had your IUD removed and told your doctor you would like more children, did you not?"

"That was years later!" I answered in exasperation.

"If you wanted more children, why then, did you ask your doctor to refer you for a tubal ligation and then cancel the operation when you were offered a date for the procedure?"

Looking at the jury, the opponent folded his arms across his chest, tut-tutted, and shook his head from side to side theatrically as he said, "It looks to me like you don't know what you want."

It suddenly made sense. What it had all been about. His line of questioning had been nothing more than a build up to facilitate that one line to the jury. He'd rehearsed it, I could tell. Too far down the road of recrimination to change his intended course, he'd had to continue, even though his interrogation hadn't come up with the goods.

"Excuse me?" I said, angrily.

"You will be excused when you have answered all my questions," the opponent snapped back.

If there was a moment in the day, where I was at risk of losing my shit, this was it. I thought of letting anger have its say. Then thought better of it.

"The IUD was over ten years old and had to be removed. I probably did say to my doctor at the time I wasn't ready for sterilisation, I would have loved more children had my circumstances been right. Time moved on and I was getting to an age when women made such decisions. I wasn't in a long-term relationship and didn't anticipate that changing. It made sense, at the time, to settle with what I had and not think about it anymore," I said calmly.

"If that was the case, why did you cancel the procedure?"

"Because the date I was given coincided with my tonsillectomy. I hadn't been in a hurry to re-book it because I was so ill after having my tonsils out, I couldn't face another medical procedure. Then I found out I was HIV-positive and it didn't matter anymore. I intended to live out what life I had left on my own."

It hadn't played out the way the opponent had wanted. Intrigued, the jurors looked from me to him and back again, wondering what was going to happen next.

"No further questions, Your Honour," the opponent said.

The judge turned to me. "Is there anything else you would like to say before the hearing concludes?"

"Yes, there is."

It was all in the timing. I waited a moment until all eyes were on me before turning my gaze towards the jury stand. One by one, I looked at all the faces in it, and said, "Thank you, for your time and for listening."

Then I looked the opponent in the eye and smiled at him, sweetly. Sickly sweet.

It was over. With a click and a snap, the opponent's laptop lid was shut. I could leave.

52

In a courtroom, I knew boundaries had to be pushed with witnesses to get to the truth. The guiding principle of the law was innocent until proven guilty and quite rightly so. However, being on the receiving end of the mockery and bullying didn't feel very fair. It seemed to me justice worryingly depended on the not necessarily reliable debating skills and emotional robustness of an already vulnerable person.

And that was me, I was that vulnerable person in the witness box. I might have managed to front out my day in court, but it still left me with a lot of negative emotions I had to deal with after it was all over.

Not taking it personally proved to be difficult. I had to stop myself from having hateful thoughts towards the opponent. It was insane, I loathed him and I didn't even know him. The opponent had been a character in the Test of Believability show, performed by someone I hadn't really met.

I had been escorted back to my playroom after the opponent had finished with me.

"Stay put for a while," Linda had said. "We'll wait until it all calms down out there and then I'll take you home."

She left to check out what was happening at the front of the building. On my own, I sat, milling over how I felt about all that had happened that day.

Carolyn walked in the room, smiling as she said, "That went well."

I looked up at her from where I was sitting and didn't smile back.

"How is it, I became the one being judged? How is what happened in there, allowed in a court of law?" I asked.

"You were not being judged, you were being assessed as a reliable witness. That's how it works," Carolyn said.

"Is he still here?" I asked.

"Who? Mark?" Carolyn asked, puzzled.

"No, not Mark, that man. Christ, I don't even know his name, and no one stopped him from doing that to me? How can that be right?"

Carolyn sighed as she pulled up a chair and sat down beside me.

"The defence barrister left the courtroom and the building the minute he had finished cross-examining you. He'll be on his train now, going home, and will not be thinking about you. He's probably reading a paper and looking forward to his dinner when he gets in. This is his job, nothing more."

"The termination. Did you know he was going to use that?" I asked.

"Yes," Carolyn replied.

"Oh my God, Carolyn! Why didn't you tell me!"

"For a couple of reasons. Firstly, I was worried you wouldn't take the stand if you knew. And secondly, I decided the element of surprise was worth the risk, and it was. It paid off. Your response was excellent."

"Thank you very much, nice of you to say so," I said sarcastically, and I didn't do sarcasm.

"Look, I know you're upset, but try to think of it in a different way. Do you not think he did you a favour?"

"I know what you are going to say, but it's going to take me a while before I can feel anything towards him other than anger. Grateful, is a bit of a far stretch."

"The jurors looked horrified. Did you notice?" asked Carolyn.

"Yes, I did," I replied. "But that didn't make me feel any better at the time."

"That, Sarah, is all that matters."

"The judge likes me, I still can't believe he let that happen. I was waiting for him to stop it and he didn't. He let me down," I said, fighting back tears.

"Don't get upset, please don't," Carolyn said. "He didn't let you down. Do you not think there was a reason why he let it continue? Think about it, at the end of the day, how it all looked from the jury's point of view."

"I suppose you're right. You know what you're doing. I am just so shocked it was like that."

"And that was exactly what I wanted. Believe it or not, he's not the most brutal I've ever come across. There are things I would have used against you, had I been the defence barrister, that he didn't."

I looked at Carolyn, measuring her up, unsure how I felt about what she had just said. I liked her, as a person, and didn't want to think of her as the ruthless defence barrister she probably once had been.

"Then thank God you were prosecuting and not defending Mark," I said, and meant it.

I had not got off lightly, but apparently should still have felt thankful for the small mercies I had been shown, because it could have been a whole lot worse.

Rubbing salt into my wounds, Mark's defence had been provided by an established HIV charitable organisation. It seemed to me, in their crusade against prosecution, they had forgotten I was HIV-positive too.

The difference being, their client had decided my fate for me.

53

By the end of the week, the judge was ready to address the jury and do his summing up. It was anticipated a verdict would be reached within the day and if this was the case, I didn't want to be at home on my own when I received the news, whichever way it went.

I wanted to be with Linda and Joe, and they were in the court building so I was there too, back in my little playroom. Down the central corridor of the victim suite, the doors to all the rooms off it were wedged open to let air circulate around the building. Directly across the corridor from the playroom was an office.

There was only one person in the small room, a woman in a court official's uniform, sitting behind a desk. She was typing, her eyes looking straight ahead at the computer screen in front of her. Every now and again the clicking on her keyboard stopped as she glanced down at the phone on her desk. Her concentration broken, she would lightly drum her fingertips on the desktop next to it, as if her mind kept wandering onto something other than her emails. I didn't know her, but I suspected she too was preoccupied with what was going on in the building that day.

Linda was the only person allowed back in the courtroom and I wouldn't see her again until it was all over. She felt strongly that I should have been in there with her, that I was entitled, and had been disappointed when the request was refused by the judge. I didn't mind though, I didn't want to go back into the courtroom. I had done my part. All I needed now was to be somewhere safe and private when the verdict came in.

My assumption had been correct about the court official. When she spoke to Joe it was without moving away from her desk, the opposite doorways being close enough to talk through them.

"I've just received a message. This is it. The jury's out."

Joe and I were the only people in the playroom. Linda did not want to leave the courtroom in case something happened in her absence. Throughout the course of the morning, other officers had appeared then left, sensing I didn't want too many people around me.

Joe stayed though and sometimes we talked, I enjoyed hearing about his plans for retirement the following year, the conversation relieving the tension of the waiting. I had brought a book and Joe had his newspaper, although neither of us managed to read for very long. After a while, we both just sat in silence with our thoughts, Joe rubbing his chin and the side of his face, the way men did when they were worried.

Sitting in the quiet, the commotion couldn't be missed. Suddenly there was noise and activity, like a wind had swept through the place, waking the building up. I could hear voices and doors opening and closing as people talked and moved about. The phone rang in the office over the corridor. Still at her desk, the woman's hand pounced on it.

I watched her listening intently to what she was being told, the receiver pressed firmly to her ear, before putting it back down in its holder. She leant over her desk so she could see me through the gaps in the doorways, and said, "It's in. You've done it."

Joe and I stood up at the same time and stared at her as she took a breath before speaking again. "It's guilty."

Joe turned his head to look at me as he asked, "Did I hear that right?" I nodded and Joe, elated at the news, picked me up and swung me around in a circle.

My little room was suddenly full of people. Linda and Carolyn were back from the courtroom, and senior police officers arrived to deliver statements to the reporters who had been waiting at the front of the court building all day. People wanted to shake my hand and talk to me. Carolyn laughed and shook her head in surprise at my shyness.

"Don't tell me, you don't know what to say. I've seen quite a few witnesses being cross-examined but not many who handled it like you did."

"Really? I felt as if the jury was on my side, but thought it was just because they felt sorry for me. Were you surprised at all, at the verdict?" I asked, curious in a 'what goes on behind the scenes' kind of way.

"No," Carolyn replied. "Not at all."

"Not at all?" I asked.

"I knew it was all going to be okay in the second half, after that recess. I don't know what happened, but you came back a different person. Very impressive."

"Thank you," I said, blushing a little.

"Don't thank me. You did all the work. You captivated them with your story. The jurors didn't take their eyes off you for a second. This is one case, I won't forget. Some stay with you, you know, the important ones," Carolyn said, as she turned to wander off and talk to other people in the room.

"And by the way," she said in a mock hushed whisper as she left, "Barristers don't normally hang out with witnesses after court in playrooms. Have you noticed how many people are here? It's for you, Sarah, all for you. Everyone in the building was rooting for you."

Linda, on her own at the other end of the room, leant against the doorframe as she silently watched me move around the room being introduced to people. As she patiently waited her turn to speak to me, I caught her eye and smiled at her. Linda smiled back and nodded while trying to fight back a tear. Not quite managing it, she quickly scooped up the escapee with the sleeve of her blouse before anyone saw.

Eventually, everyone left the playroom and it was just us.

"Come on," Linda said. "Let's get you home. You've got birthday cake to eat."

"How do you know it's Livvy's birthday? I don't remember mentioning it," I asked, following her out the room.

"The judge told me," Linda replied.

"The judge told you? How come?" I asked, confused.

"The judge told everybody in the courtroom, in his summing up for the jury. God, I wish you could have heard it. I cried. Everybody bloody cried."

"What did he say?"

Linda stopped walking and turned around to face me. "He said, that you were brave. That he respected you. That you were a good person and a good mother. He told the jury it was a special day for you and it had fallen on your daughter's birthday, he'd remembered Livvy's date of birth from your file. He told them to do the right thing, on this day, of all days. He basically told them Sarah, that he thinks you are fucking incredible."

"Wow. That was really nice of him," I said, taken aback and touched at the same time by what Linda had told me.

"Nice of him?" Linda laughed. "I'll say. It took the jury less than two hours to reach a unanimous verdict of 'guilty' and I reckon, they were sitting playing Scrabble for most of that."

Back at home, Eve called in to see me. "What next?" she asked.

I shrugged my shoulders while I thought about it, then answered her question. "I suppose I had better get on with writing something for the press."

After the verdict, the local press had immediately requested an interview, no doubt seeking details of the case they were not allowed to use without my consent. Nothing sold papers better than the tantalising suggestion of sex or death and HIV stories had the potential for both.

I declined the offer of interviews and wrote a response to the verdict instead, which was submitted to the press via the police. It was a statement about the importance of honesty regarding HIV and testing at the beginning of relationships. There was nothing personal in the text, only the wish to express my gratitude to all involved who had helped me find out the truth.

I was not confident all or any it would be used. It wouldn't have surprised me if the press had considered the content rather dry and boring. However, the released statement from a woman known only as 'X' appeared in print both locally and nationally.

My words, as my daughter gleefully told me, even made it into *The Times*.

54

It came out in the trial, Mark believed what he had done to me, had been done to him too. Whether a reason, pardon, or an excuse, the jury had made their decision.

Many years before me, and Kate, and other women Mark had been in relationships with, he had met a woman who he believed had changed his life. She was African, wanted to stay in the country and in order to do so, had wanted Mark to marry her. This was the way Mark had explained it to me once, towards the end of our relationship. I remembered wondering why he was telling me, at the time unaware of her significance.

Mark had felt there was something he should know that she wasn't telling him. He sensed he was being lied to. He refused to marry her and she left him. He had no proof, other than his own intuition, that she was the source of his HIV. When Linda told me about this, it felt like another piece of the puzzle had dropped into place. I surmised, Mark was probably right. The feeling of something being wrong, I knew well.

Mark did not want his HIV status confirmed. Only at the insistence of a woman he was in a relationship with, did Mark finally agreed to have the test. Pushed into it by his then partner, he didn't want to but eventually and begrudgingly agreed to it, basically because she made the appointment for him, took him, sat with him and made sure he did it. Her motives were sincere; she had tested positive and cared enough about Mark to want him to be on treatment too.

Mark regularly and reliably took the medication he needed for two years while he was still with her, then stopped when he met me. Not immediately, but he was on wind-down. Missed appointments to collect his prescription became more frequent. When he did attend his clinic, he became increasingly more difficult, complaining a lot and being rude to staff. He caused problems by making a big fuss about things, such as waiting his turn with other people in the waiting room, in case someone recognised him.

Mark's attitude led staff to believe he was bitter and resentful of his diagnosis. He gained a reputation for being unreasonable and uncooperative. He refused point-blank throughout the entire time of his treatment to discuss any partners, past or present.

By the time I had seroconverted, the clinic staff had not seen or heard from Mark for months. Telephone messages went unanswered and letters posted to his own house left unopened. The clinic did not have my address in their database because they did not know Mark had moved in with me. I didn't exist because Mark had never told them about me.

The irony of it was, if it hadn't been for Mark's rudeness, he may well have gone unnoticed by Eve and I would never have found out the truth.

Staff at Mark's clinic talked about him negatively because no one wanted to work with him. For this reason, they took it in turns to see him. In brief, people at his clinic did not like him. His expectation of preferential treatment and the arrogance that went with it became well known and talk of his behaviour reached other centres, including Eve's.

I know that name, she had thought, way back when I had told her I had been in a relationship with him.

All of the information from Mark's medical records became evidence for the prosecution in the trial, backed up with testimonies from the health professionals who had tried to help him. Everything was recorded, from his absences at the clinic to his attitude. The stark reality of how Mark presented as a person, was very different to the person Joe had interviewed after his arrest.

There was no reality in deception. Romanticising the whole situation that was the relationship his lies were built on, Mark had claimed he hadn't disclosed his HIV status in the beginning for fear of losing me. He had stated on record, he'd believed it would work out between us because he had intended to spend the rest of his life with me. The word 'denial' wasn't mentioned until much later, suggested by his defence barrister.

As distasteful as I found Mark's limp explanation for all that had happened, I was prepared to concede that his reasons may well have been fluid and interchangeable throughout the duration of our relationship. It was possible at times, he liked the idea of us united together in our HIV status and at other times, horrified to find himself thinking in such a way.

Personally, I preferred to consider the real problem that caused all the unhappiness was how much Mark must have disliked himself to pretend to be someone he wasn't, the whole time I was with him. The effort that must have gone into the deceit was deserving of some sort of warped recognition because I was completely fooled.

It must have been soul destroying and maybe living a lie did that to a person. Removed the essence of who they really were and left in its place a cold, empty shell.

I was asked in court, if I would've stayed with Mark had he told me about his HIV and my answer received a lot of coverage in the press. The way it read was misleading because, in truth, there was no correct answer.

My response wasn't the problem, the question was. Mark telling me he was HIV-positive never happened. Carolyn was talking about a person who did not exist.

Had I been asked about an honest and brave man who was the one for me and had told me he was HIV-positive, my answer would have been simple. There was no doubt in my mind, I would have still fallen in love and built a future with a person who had principles and qualities I admired.

All the doubt had rested with Mark. Unable to see the kindness and warmth in other people, Mark had based his assumptions on himself, denying me any opportunity to show him a different way to be.

It wasn't about forgiving Mark for being HIV-positive, the way it had come across in the papers. It was about living with hope rather than regret. Living a life, not a lie.

English law had ruled many years before Mark and I met, that the reckless transmission of HIV was a criminal offence. Mark was the first person in the country following this initial test case, to be convicted on entering a 'not guilty' plea. He received the maximum prison sentence the judge was able to give him.

The day after his sentencing in court, a story appeared on the front pages of local newspapers, containing an interview with someone claiming to be Mark's partner. She talked about how herself and Mark had known each other for some time, their love rekindling after his arrest.

I was surprised to read this person felt proud of Mark for standing up in court and facing up to all the mistakes he had made, neither of which he had done. I also found it strange how someone felt able to represent Mark and speak for him, an individual confident enough to seek the attention of the press, even though they had not been present and therefore privy to the proceedings of a case tried in a closed court.

I don't suppose this was the intention but it worked out in my favour. Speculation on who the mystery woman 'X' was, an accolade I was never interested in, became yesterday's news. Replacing any interest there might have been regarding Mark's sentencing, the press ran a story featuring someone eager to talk about her relationship with Mark and regardless of the fact he had also infected her with HIV, she had forgiven him and was standing by her man.

Some people, understandably confused by everything about the case that had been printed in the tabloids, mistakenly believed myself and this person to be one and the same and this was disappointing. With wildly opposing views on Mark's behaviour and everything I had done to try and stop it, I would have preferred it recognised that myself and this person were two very different women.

The words of support in the article, as loving as they were, also clarified my endeavours had been for good reason. After his relationship with me, nothing had changed. Mark continued to be a perpetrator. His HIV-positive partner had confirmed it, in writing, printed by the press.

After the trial, Mark featured in persistent dreams I would have. Waking up confused and upset, I looked for answers, disturbed by the way my mind seemed to be playing tricks on me. I read about a strange phenomenon called Stockholm Syndrome, which under different circumstances I would have struggled to understand but because of my dreams, it struck a chord.

Victims emotionally bonding with their abuser was a survival strategy well recognised in psychology, I found out, giving me some sort of explanation. While I was sleeping, Mark was the Ticket Master on the express train taking me somewhere I didn't want to go, but I had no choice. His journey was my journey.

The dreams were always the same, the last remaining ghost-like fragment of Mark in my mind. They catapulted to a time after his incarceration and he had changed, he cared about other people. In my unconscious mind, he was a person capable of feeling genuine regret for his actions and he was sorry. In every dream I had, he told me so.

How very, very sorry he was, for everything.

EPILOGUE

The year I moved away from the small town I was born in, was the same year Mark was released from prison. He served about the same amount of time the investigation into his behaviour took. Not that how much time he spent in prison was important to me. Along with some sort of recognition he understood how wrong his actions were and validation it would stop, all I wanted was the truth.

The last I ever heard about him was he preferred to go by a different name and lived anonymously in a remote coastal village somewhere in the country. To all accounts, it sounded like a single, solitary existence suited Mark and I agreed with his choice of post-trial lifestyle. Unless narcissists were able to gain enough self-awareness to un-narcissist themselves, it was in everyone's best interests they settled for the malignant relationship they had with their egos and didn't bother anybody else. If this was the future path Mark had taken, I wished him the best of British with it.

The relationship I had with Robin eventually came to an end. Shortly after the trial, we called it a day on being a couple. Even though, other than the early days, we never really were one. The things that had worked thoroughly well long distance, never quite translated when we were in the same country together. Robin wanted the person he had met and I had changed.

Robin also wanted children and this would prey on my mind when we were together. I didn't want to be the reason why Robin never got to be a father. He would still ask, and as much as I felt for him, all the conversations did was reinforce how different our lives were.

Luckily, during one of his longer spells back at home in France, Robin got someone else pregnant. This meant I didn't have to say the words to end the relationship, which would have made me feel terrible. Robin had wanted a family of his own and I was happy for him. Robin, my dear friend, lives in his home town with his partner and twin girls.

I call in to see Eve and Alex when I go home. They still work, "in that mucky place," as Eve's mother calls it, supporting and caring for people. For all they did for me, I think of them both with much affection and gratitude and don't suppose that will ever change.

I didn't see Linda again after the trial. We said we would keep in touch but maybe for the right reasons, we never contacted each other and Linda became part of my past. I would imagine she is climbing the ranks of her police force and like Carolyn, still manages to do the school run most mornings.

I hope Joe, on retiring, sometimes sits in his garden with a glass of wine and remembers the rosy-cheeked pretty woman he spun around in a courthouse, once. I also hope Linda is sitting next to him. I always thought they would've made a lovely couple.

Livvy finished university and put her English degree to good use pursuing a career in writing. She settled in the same city she studied in and started looking for ways to make new friends. A cause close to her heart, Livvy volunteered some of her time to a charity that provided play therapy for children affected by HIV. She met her partner there, who told her on their first date, he was HIV-positive.

My children are all grown up now. When Livvy and Sam look back at everything that happened during their childhood, I hope they think of their mother as the woman who always got back up, no matter how hard life knocked her down. I hope, they are as proud of me, as I am of them.

My parents never found out about my diagnosis. In the years following it, my decision not to tell them never wavered. Not once, was I ever tempted or felt the need to divulge my HIV status, or the circumstances surrounding how it came about.

The year my dad died, I started writing and once I started, I couldn't stop. My words and my story became a book. Finally, I'd had my say, my way. My mum has no idea of the events that transpired, described in its pages. Thankfully, she is content in the knowledge all is well with her youngest daughter and doesn't need to know any more than that.

When we are together, she enjoys herself chatting on about normal things. It is just as well talking about the weather and her neighbours in mind-boggling detail isn't illegal, otherwise, my mum would be straight in the slammer doing time for being a happy old lady.

I had an interesting relationship with my writing. I laughed a little and cried a lot, as I worked my way through all the poignant moments of my past. Revisiting it wasn't easy. My emotions often caught me off guard. There were occasions when sitting alone with my laptop in front of me, I wondered whether it was a good idea to continue tapping away at the keys, my reservation for good reason. At times, it felt like I was prodding at an old wound, I should be leaving well alone.

Yet still, I felt compelled to keep going, even when it left me feeling vulnerable and exposed. Slowly these feelings started to fade and eventually, completely stopped. My writing evolved into something very different, it became a liberating experience. The more I wrote the better it felt, in many ways a process of healing and growth for me and one I wanted to share.

After my diagnosis an HIV-positive friend would have made a difference, a connection with someone who knew how it felt, but I was too scared to do anything about it. I like that anyone who wants to meet me, can. I'm right here in these pages because I put a little piece of my heart into each and every one.

Perhaps the final part of my story was to write it down. When I had finished the last chapter, I found any lingering fear that may have been hanging around, had gone. Exploring how I felt in writing had somehow set me free. I learnt a lot about myself and was free to be whoever I wanted to be.

The best bit of all was, I discovered, I was quite happy being me.

A very real and perfect woman, as my partner keeps on telling me. I did get that long-term relationship I always thought I wasn't capable of after all, notably after I became HIV-positive. Perhaps there is a depth to me now because of my past, a strength and attractiveness that far outmeasures physical appearance alone.

When the anniversary of my diagnosis reached double figures and beyond, a statement of hope was finally released that changed the definition of what it means to live with HIV.

Undetectable equals untransmittable. U=U. The symbol that represents so much to HIV-positive people.

Countries all over the world have endorsed the statement and the message is growing. Our bodies aren't dangerous. We can make a baby without artificial alternatives because we can make love without the shame and fear of passing on the virus. We want to take care of ourselves and our partners. We want to and can, end this epidemic, together.

And then there's all this talk of a cure. There always has been but it feels like it's getting closer. When those clever scientists finally find it, which they will, what a time in history it will be, and I fully intend to be around to see it. Until then, being HIV-positive is part of who I am and without the experiences I have had in my life, I wouldn't be me.

I am kind to myself these days; I don't bash myself up with destructive thoughts, the way I did all those years ago. I wasn't really an empty painted mannequin, I never became Buffalo Lady because I didn't grow a hump, and I wasn't a tragic mermaid because I'm still here. These strange creatures existed only in my mind because I created them and put them there.

When I think about the past, I feel like leaping back in time and giving myself a great big hug and telling me everything is going to be just fine, because it is. There was never any such thing as an old life and a new life, it was always me.

All I needed was the faith to get past the fragility of human nature and find myself again

Everyone has secrets.

The only person you ever truly know, is yourself.

ABOUT THE AUTHOR

Annie grew up in the North East of England and now lives in the South East. *This New Life* is her first novel.